OTHER BOOKS IN ENGLISH TRANSLATION

BY FAHMIDA RIAZ

Godavari

FORTRESS OF THE FORGOTTEN ONES

Originally published in Urdu as *Qila-e-Faramoshi* by Oxford University Press, Pakistan

Published by agreement with the estate of Fahmida Riaz

First edition, 2026

Library in Congress Cataloging-in-Publication: Available Upon Request.

Paperback ISBN: 978-1-960385-51-2

Ebook ISBN: 978-1-960385-52-9

Support for the publication of this book provided by Armory Square Ventures.

Armory Square Ventures

Cover design by Armory Square Ventures

Interior design by Kaija Straumanis

Open Letter is the University of Rochester's nonprofit, literary translation press.

500 Joseph C. Wilson Blvd.

Morey Hall 303,

Rochester NY 14627

www.openletterbooks.org

Printed in the United States.

FORTRESS OF THE FORGOTTEN ONES

BY FAHMIDA RIAZ

Translated from the Urdu by Sana R. Chaudhry

OPEN LETTER

For all Parsis living in Hindustan, Pakistan, and the rest of the world, whose earliest beliefs laid the foundation for modern faiths, cultures, and traditions.

Were my tribute to be accepted, how greatly it would honor and dignify me

Dedicated to the postmen,
to the coachmen,
to the railway workers.
Dedicated to the hungry, brave men of the mill,
to the farmer—Sovereign of the World,
Governor of All Things,
Viceroy of God on Earth—
whose cattle were herded away by tyrants,
whose daughter was abducted by dacoits,
Who lost one finger's breadth
from a handful of land to the patwari,
And another to the sarkar in the name of tax.

Faiz Ahmad Faiz
Sar-e-Wadi-e-Sina

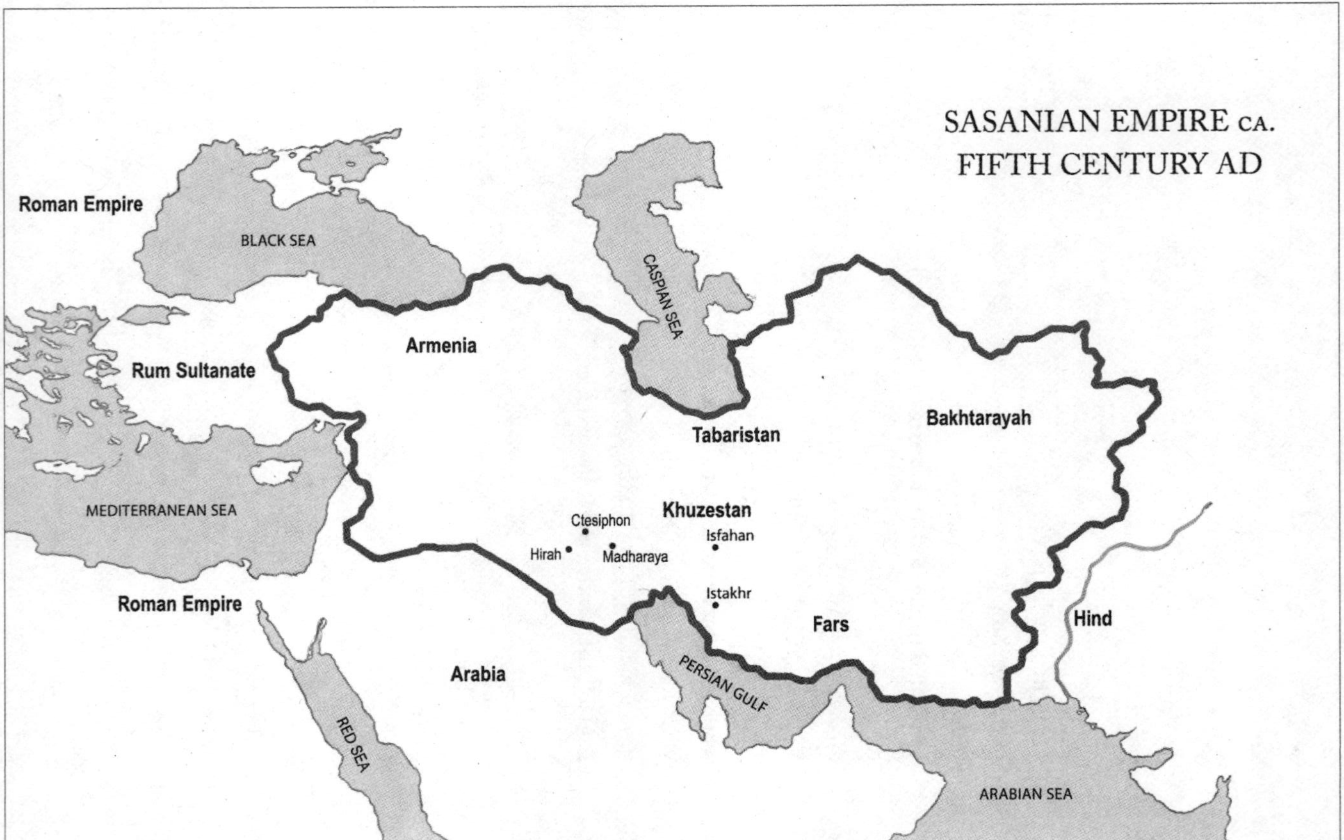
SASANIAN EMPIRE CA.
FIFTH CENTURY AD
Roman Empire
BLACK SEA
CASPIAN SEA
Armenia
Rum Sultanate
Tabaristan
Bakhtarayah
MEDITERRANEAN SEA
Ctesiphon
Khuzestan
Isfahan
Hirah
Madharaya
Istakhr
Roman Empire
Fars
Hind
Arabia
PERSIAN GULF
RED SEA
ARABIAN SEA

TABLE OF CONTENTS

A MINOR DEBT

(A few facts about the novel)

> The seeker's heart still presses for its due;
>
> There lingers, upon the nail, a debt to this knot half-undone.
>
> —Ghalib

Such were the feelings that moved the writer to pen this novel. Since we were young, we had heard Mazdak's name regarded as the first socialist revolutionary in history, and of Iranian descent. But people know little about who he was, the circumstances that gave birth to his movement, what paths it took that shaped it, how it spread, and how it ultimately came to an end. Then there is another question: why, compared to other historical figures, is there so little known about Mazdak? The answer to this last question quickly becomes clear in the early phases of historical research: all historians are in agreement over one fact: any information about Mazdak and his socialist revolution has been deliberately suppressed by chroniclers of his time, and when they had no choice but to mention him, it was only briefly, and in a negative light. This ensured that the historians who came after couldn't even find the scant information that might have aided them in furthering their research. Thus, Mazdak gradually faded from the pages of history.

What's marvelous is that this story is very old. Mazdak's era belongs to the fifth century AD, only four hundred years after the birth of Prophet Isa (Peace Be Upon Him). Just before this period lies the time span from Prophet Musa (Peace Be Upon Him) back to Prophet Ibrahim (Peace Be Upon Him), a time when the boundaries between history and anthropology blur, and where the preceding eras don't end abruptly but merge into new ones, continuing to flow alongside them (in fact, it is entirely possible that they persist even now in some faraway mountain settlement in Sindh). Painting a picture of Mazdak's life and circumstances becomes all the more difficult when we consider that, between then and now, the geographical landscape of the places where these events unfolded has been altered many times. The cities and provinces that existed in the fifth century AD have been destroyed repeatedly, their borders redrawn numerous times, and they are no longer known by their original names.

But when I set out on my search, one door after another opened into a whole new world. Alongside Mazdak's revolution, this story also became a tale of the origin of a culture and tradition from this region whose ancient roots spread far and wide in past centuries, and whose legacy continues into our present moment. The first thing we learn is that in Mazdak's time, the Zoroastrian religion prevailed in the Persian empire—the oldest religion in history to be "formally and duly" instituted. Zoroastrianism and Hinduism share so many similarities that it is difficult to determine which came first. Historians are of the view that during the age of the Vedas, the religion (or religions) practiced in Hindustan were the earliest, but the discrepancy that soon emerges—and what is becoming evident to us today—is that the Zoroastrian faith is considerably older. Another important point to bear in mind is that the Aryas lived in Iran, and that the region derived its name from them. (Past kings of Iran also adopted the title "Aryamehr.")

Thus, this novel is the outcome of tireless research carried out over the course of two to two and a half years. The following resources have assisted me:

1. *The Shahnameh*

First, I decided to consult the world-renowned *Shahnameh* by Ferdowsi. A Persian poet of the tenth century AD, Abolqasem Ferdowsi (940–1020 AD) is famous not only for composing *The Shahnameh*—a masnavi of over fifty thousand verses and the longest epic in the world by a single author—but also as a reputable historian of ancient Iran, whose works are frequently referenced by chroniclers from both eastern and western traditions. *The Shahnameh* is not easily available in Pakistan, but I discovered a copy in the Pakistan Academy of Letters (Islamabad), which contained a few pages devoted to Mazdak and his socialist revolution. However, *The Shahnameh* is above all a dastan of illustrious kings, and its treatment of Mazdak is cursory at best. Nonetheless, it offers an intriguing and informed account of the final chapter of Mazdak's life, which allowed me to make use of it in this novel.

2. *The Avesta*

The Zoroastrian people, who date back thousands of years, did not simply vanish from the face of the earth. They continue to migrate and settle in the subcontinent, and our "Parsi community" is, in fact, Zoroastrian. The name of their holy book is *The Avesta*, which is still read by Parsis today. This book provided me with material on Zoroastrian hymns, such as *hamds* (a literary genre exclusively for praising God), *naats* (a literary genre exclusively for praising the Prophet), and other related material.

Having acquired this foundational material, we then turn to the landscape in which the Mazdakite revolution took root and spread—the Persian empire—and then we must consider what was that landscape like.

At the time when Mazdak was born, the Iranian tribe or dynasty that had been ruling the Persian sultanate for more than four hundred years was known as "Sasanians." It was a magnificent empire, a vast dominion whose borders touched Hindustan on one side and met the frontiers of Arab and Roman sultanates on the other, with whom they were always locked in combat. These borders were in constant flux—at times the Romans seized these regions, and at other times the Iranians regained control. Jerusalem was one such territory, where Jewish communities had settled even before the Sasanians arrived, and where part of the Torah was composed. On another frontier were the White Huns, who often launched attacks on the Iranian empire.

There were the forces shaping the Iranian kingdom, the "circumstances of the time" in which Mazdak struggled to advance his socialist movement. In tracing these circumstances, several sources proved useful; for although we were not given a definitive timeline of the Mazdakite revolution, to a discerning eye it becomes clear that: My dastan lies scattered all over the garden.

3. The Bible

I was able to find details about the circumstances of that period easily in the Old Testament, which mentions the Iranian empire in two of its chapters.

4. *History of the Arabs* by Philip Hitti

By Mazdak's time, a small kingdom known as "Hirah" had been established in the Arab lands. It paid taxes to the Iranian empire and also maintained ties with the Roman—later Byzantine—empire. Bedouin tribes and family dynasties had settled across the rest of the Arab region. For centuries they had attacked the Iranian empire and, at times, had even taken up residence there. I found reliable information about their habits and ways, their social life, and their customs and traditions in Lebanese author Philip Hitti's book *History of the Arabs*. The verses recited by the Bedouins in this novel come from this book. Philip Hitti was an Arab Christian from Lebanon whose mother tongue was Arabic, and he had easy access to ancient manuscripts and texts. (I have yet to encounter a better work on Arab history.)

5. *The History of al-Tabari*

Known by his rather long name of "Allama abi Ja'far Muhammad bin Jarir al-Tabari," this historian from the ninth and tenth century AD is held in high esteem throughout the world. In the second volume of his *History of al-Tabari* (also known as *History of the Prophets and Kings*), I found a wealth of reliable material on Iran, the Arab lands, and Rum. It also contains references to the White Huns, which gave me valuable insights into the Hun tribes and their relations with the Persian kings, proving particularly helpful for this novel.

6. *The Lands of the Eastern Caliphate* by G. Le Strange

This incomparable historical book is also mentioned in the renowned writer Qurratulain Hyder's autobiography *Kaar-e-Jahaan*

Daraaz Hai (*The Task of the World is Long*). It proved especially valuable in shaping the literary landscape of this novel because it presents the full political topography—complete with maps—of the Arab conquest of Iran. Although the Arabs changed the names of certain cities over the course of a century, many of the names of cities, provinces, and rivers remained in use in the Persian empire.

7. *L'Iran Sous Le Sassanides* by Dr. Arthur Christensen

The authority of all sources mentioned above is indisputable, but this novel *Qila-e-Faramoshi* (قلعۂ فراموشی) could never have been written if this book had not been my guiding light. It was written by well-known Danish Orientalist and expert linguist Dr. Arthur Christensen. His book is a rigorous study of the cultures and traditions during the Sasanian period, and it allowed me to frame the novel with confidence. In addition to informing me about marriage and divorce customs, it also offered insights into the kind of foods eaten in that era, how it was cooked, the clothing worn, the fabrics from which they were made, and the styles of jewelry common at the time.

All these sources have enabled me to present before you a novel grounded almost entirely on historical facts, with one or two exceptions. Even its most significant dialogues are historically accurate, for I have preserved the language of the times. For example, the royal sergeant's proclamation in the King's court, the King's words in Mazdak's support, and Mazdak's own account of his apostleship and aspirations—all of these are detailed in the book. Thus, I did not need to recreate these conversations using my imagination. This is why I stand firmly behind the authenticity of the evidence I offer you in this novel.

8. The History of Ancient Hind

Another element that came into contact with the Sasanian empire and played a key role in shaping the neighboring countries was the tribe known as the "White Huns," or "Hunan" in Sanskrit.

They are mentioned both in the history of ancient Hind as well as *al-Tabari*. Tabari uses the word "Hebdali" (from the original "Hephthali," since the sounds *p* and *ph* do not occur in the Arabic language). These were polyandrous tribes, meaning that one woman could take multiple husbands. (Their long-standing presence in Hindustan for thousands of years recalls the famous Indian historical character Draupadi and her many husbands, suggesting that this may have been a region inhabited by the White Huns, from whom this custom first spread. It remains in practice in certain remote mountainous areas even today.)

9. The History of the Jews

We found the history of the Jews in the Old Testament, while the New Testament offered a reliable record of the lifestyle, customs, and preoccupations of the Christians during that time. Although numerous books exist on these subjects, I selected the Bible and its annotations as my primary sources.

10. The Internet

It would be ungrateful to not acknowledge the invaluable treasure contained in the multitudes of online archives that helped me refine the details on every page of this novel. They were so many that recording each one is impossible.

11. The Novelist's Imagination and Creative Impulse

Since this is a novel, my imagination has naturally played a part in its composition. I had to transform the figures found in these historical records into real people, who speak, who laugh, who err, who dream. Thus, a few characters make an appearance in the novel who are creations of my own imagination. The mind of a historical fiction writer also plays a part in connecting the dots—for instance, several sources note that a fortress of the forgotten ones really existed in the Iranian empire, but where? According to Dr. Christensen, a similar fortress was situated in Khuzestan, where the Khuz tribes lived. For a long time now, no province by this name has existed. In another source, I read that the Arab conquerors had begun to call "Khuz" tribes by the name "Huz." An idea struck me: if "Huz" were written in its plural form following the rules of the Arabic alphabet, would it not become "Ahvaz"? With anticipation, I turned the pages of *The Lands of the Eastern Caliphate* to search for "Ahvaz," and was thrilled to find that the Arab conquerors often found the architecture of ancient Iran astonishing. The book also mentions a fortress where political prisoners were kept. Thus I came to believe that such a fortress truly existed, and understood that it must have been located in or around Ahvaz. Who knows, perhaps its traces still stand today!

Historical records also tell us that Mazdak's socialist revolution lasted seven years. This raises the question: how could such a movement take root in such a powerful, magnificent empire? Yet when we consider the circumstances of the time, the answer becomes clear—Mazdak had support from the reigning king and his royal army, whose influence the nobles, religious leaders, and priests sought to curtail. The king and his army, in turn, needed the support of the Mazdakite cause to preserve their own authority, which enjoyed favor among the great majority of poor subjects. Once the struggle between the kingdom's formidable powers—the aristocrats, the priests, the royal army, and the king—came to an end, the crown no longer had any use for Mazdak. The king's successor, his son Nosherwan, wasted no time in eliminating Mazdak and his followers.

My "labor of love" now lies before you, for whatever it's worth. But it will surely give the discerning reader something to ponder.

Fahmida Riaz
Karachi

CHAPTER 1

In the Khuzestan province of ancient Persia stood a mighty fortress called "Gēlgard." It was known as "Andmishn" in the Armenian language. Used to detain those political prisoners who were meant to be erased from public memory, it was also called "Anushbard," which means "Fortress of the Forgotten Ones." As such, it was forbidden to mention not only the people who were imprisoned there, but even to utter the name of the fortress itself.

"All present in the imperial court! Observe. It is incumbent upon each and every one of you to look at those who are lesser than you—not to those with a higher rank," the royal sergeant announced. A second sergeant positioned in the center of the court recited the same words loudly, so that the viewers queued along the wall could hear the royal proclamation, which had been repeated within the royal courts of the Sasanid empire for centuries, year after year, in each king's era.

"Reflect upon the state of those who are lesser than you," said the royal sergeant, which the second sergeant repeated in a resounding voice. "Reflect, and you will find your rank to be a blessing. Those who are of lower rank should take heart in knowing that they are better than those who have been disgraced. And those who have been disgraced should look to those who have been sentenced. And those who have been sentenced . . ."

The royal sergeant recited his age-old, worn out sermon, and the second sergeant repeated it verbatim to those sitting at the back.

This was Ctesiphon, the capital of the Sasanid empire.

It was the fifth century AD.

This was the royal palace of the Aryan kingdom. The walls of its vast, sweeping court were draped in exquisite silks and inlaid with mosaics of crystal, rubies, and emeralds. The floors were laid with the thickest silk carpets. Dignitaries of the kingdom were seated on chairs adorned with diamonds and jewels according to rank. Heeding the royal proclamation, they turned their necks in unison, casting unblinking stares at officials and courtiers of lower rank.

Before the western wall of the Great Hall, upon a throne of gold sat Qobad, King of Kings, perched on an opulent chair upholstered in plush crimson fabric. His form was concealed beneath an array of gold-threaded robes and precious gems. A crown studded with rubies and diamonds rested upon his head. Despite all this grandeur, his countenance betrayed a slight unease.

Then came the file of royal princes—Kavus, who had just come of age; the younger Prince Khosrow, whose youthful countenance revealed a sagacity beyond his years; and Zam, who was missing an eye. It was quite possible that this mischief had been caused by one of his stepmothers, since a prince with a bodily disability could never be heir to the throne. Next were the citizens of the provinces, known as the *shahān*. Then came the *wispuhrān*, members of the seven royal families who were trusted with important responsibilities, such as crowning the king. Next was a row of chairs laid out for the aristocrats and landlords of the kingdom, known as *wuzurgān*. These also included the *mobedān*, or chief priests, who were the kingdom's spiritual exemplars. The *mobedān* made decisions and held ranks of their own. Then came the *azadān*, who were nobles by birth. These included the ancestral warriors of the kingdom. Next were the *dehqanān*. They were not farmers but rather the owners of indigenous agricultural estates who collected taxes from tenant farmers. The rows of chairs came to an end with the officers. Behind the chairs a crowd of commoners sat reverently upon the carpets. There were farmers, artisans, ordinary shopkeepers; in fact, even criminals from the jails and torture cells had been summoned for this special ceremony. Not a single straw was out of place in the Sasanid court. It was a strict demarcation of class and hierarchy.

The sergeant sounded his kettledrum and commanded: "Observe you shall!"

The courtiers turned their necks once more. The sergeants continued their antiquated proclamation: "Beware! None among you may covet a rank higher than his own, bestowed upon him by right of birth . . ."

In the row of the fire-temple keepers, a mobed sitting on a jeweled chair struggled to keep himself from smiling a scornful, wry smile.

By right of birth! Mazdad thought. *The way these elites abduct common women day and night, there must be countless princes and noblemen "by right of birth" playing inside the farmers' huts this very instant. And their women—eternally enamored with the farmers' chiseled physiques—who can say with certainty how much fruit born of the farmers' seed is ripening into the elixir of youth within these palace gardens?*

Looking intently at his gold-and-silver embroidered shoes, he thought to himself: *Every single person present in court today is privy to this secret, but none of them has the courage to speak of it. So many lies! So much betrayal!* His blood boiled. *And their choruses of Yazd! The invocations of the Avesta! Beneath these pretenses lies greed, lust . . . unfathomable lust! Yes! That is all that is left now.*

The royal sergeant continues reading the scroll:

"Be content, O people of the exalted Aryan kingdom. Contentment is a noble virtue in the world. Nothing is better than contentment. Ahura Mazda declared . . . inner peace and gratitude . . . etcetera."

Ahura Mazda! What did Ahura Mazda preach, you demon! Do you remember? Have you discerned a single word, a single line of the Avesta? No! Nobody even remembers the Avesta. But Mani understood it. Unfortunate Mani, who tried to guide this mob of heretics. But his life was not spared. The mobeds had him killed . . . Ah! Mani! An artist . . . pure as the fresh winter snow. When he anointed the canvas with his brushstroke, it was as if the trees, blossoms, fruit, birds, and members of humankind were infused with the breath of life. And his script! Such an immaculate script.

Mazdad's father—Bamdad—had preserved some of Mani's writings, which he had shown only to his son. Whatever Bamdad remembered, he would recite under the cover of night. After Mani's assassination, all his disciples had gone into hiding. Some of them had left Persia, while others vowed they would keep their ideas and emotions alive, without even a soul knowing about it. Generation after generation, they maintained their silence. Bamdad was one of them. He had passed the secret down to his son, as had always been done—by oral tradition. But now, fear gnawed at him. His son, exceptionally intelligent and deeply sensitive, did not believe in silence. He was a rebel, drawn to Mani's teachings. Bamdad would tremble each time Mazdad leaned in and whispered in his ear: "That's all well and good, dear father. But in the real world we cannot walk the path of our holy saint Mani. We'll have to resort to other tactics."

This was Mazdad. A respectable mobed, he had committed the Avesta to memory—though "memorized" hardly did it justice. Each tenet was etched deep in the most private recesses of his heart, and everything he observed in his surroundings went against his understanding of the Avesta.

His surroundings . . .

He despaired as he stepped out of the imperial court with the other attendees in queues. Nothing about these surroundings resembled the past. The Aryan empire had become immense, stretching from the islands of the Persian Gulf to the land of Armenia—its reach growing with each successive king. Even the Roman empire trembled before it, having suffered defeat after defeat at the hands of the invincible Sasanid army.

But Mazdad did not care much for these conquests and defeats. To his mind, Aryan rule had existed since the beginning of time itself. Since the birth of Gayomars—the first man to walk the earth—this sultanate had been expanding and contracting. The real question for him was how the empire, large or small, was sustaining itself.

The West was ruled by the Roman empire—grander even than the Aryan realm! Yet, they too faced the same predicament. Time and again, their kings and commanders launched full-scale attacks on Aryan lands to conquer and annex them for their kingdom. But each time, they met with crushing defeat—driven back from the battlefield, leaving thousands of their dead behind. In turn, the Aryans retaliated with a series of devastating incursions into Roman territory, seizing control of their borderlands and asserting their dominance.

This bitter rivalry bred new alliances. The Roman kings and nobles became friends with Aryan kings and nobles, willingly marrying their daughters into each other's families.

If the Aryan king was dissatisfied with a person or tribe, there wasn't a more fitting place to exile them than the Roman empire. Long ago—when barely two centuries had passed—a Persian traitor, whose parents had named him Zartosht after the Great Prophet, had also been sent into exile in the Roman kingdom. He was of royal descent, and had been welcomed jubilantly by the Romans, who were no less proud than the Sasanids in matters of lineage. They called him "Bundus," since the Romans could not turn their tongues to pronounce Persian words like Zartosht, butchering them to sound like their own. Thus he came to be known as Bundus.

They say that Bundus returned to Persia, but nobody knows what became of him. What were his teachings? Perhaps that every Aryan had an equal claim to the kingdom's resources—food, water, gold, and silver. *Eliminate the divide between the rich and poor.* These were perilous ideas, sure to provoke the wrath of the King and his nobles. At first, the Roman rulers welcomed him as a traitor to the Aryan crown, an architect of discord sowing unrest within the walls of the Sasanid palace. Later, however, his dangerous ideas compelled them to send him back to Persia. They came to see that he was not merely a traitor to the Aryan crown and throne, but an insurgent against the very economic and social order upon which they depended for their own survival. And so, they sent him on his way:

"Farewell, honorable guest—go preach your sermons elsewhere."

Zoroaster's ideology—that "all are equal" and that the divide between the rich and poor must be erased—carried the seeds of explosive popularity. It was a formula for disaster, catastrophe, and the eventual overthrow of monarchy itself. The Romans hoped that these ideals would take root in the Aryan empire, wiping away every trace of its glory and grandeur from the annals of history. Then, they would easily conquer the Sasanid empire, and those proud, imperious Aryans would find themselves shining the shoes of Roman nobles and polishing the floors of their palaces.

Surroundings . . .

Mazdad took a deep breath, recalling the words of the royal sergeant.

As soon as he stepped through the towering doors of the King's majestic and forbidding palace, the surroundings lay stark before him. His two-horse chariot rolled through desolate lands. A ghastly famine gripped the kingdom. It rarely rained in these areas, but centuries ago laborers had created a network of water canals across their land utilizing the rivers so they could irrigate it year-round. The rivers were now bone-dry. The crops, ready for harvest, had withered on the stalk. Farmers had not a morsel of grain to eat. The common folk were dying of hunger. Surely the granaries of the nobles, royals, and mobeds overflowed, but not even a single straw from these stores made its way to the mouths of the starving farmers. In fact, when King Qobad suggested distributing grain from the royal storehouses and urged the wealthy to give up a share of their reserves, the nobles bristled with rage. The mobeds made their displeasure known through their tight-lipped, stiff silence. Qobad may indeed be king, but it was the mobeds and nobles who were the kingmakers. And so, the King refrained from insisting any further. He was caught in a bind.

All at once, a horde of farmers appeared out of nowhere on the deserted path. With rags clinging to their bodies, skin glued to their bones, dark hollows circling their eyes, lips parched, and arms outstretched like a mob of zombies, they lunged toward Mazdad's chariot, crying out words of adulation:

"Alms! Alms! *Peshwa!* We are hungry, Lord! We are thirsty!"

"Faster . . . drive faster. Get us far away from here," Mazdad snapped at the charioteer. The charioteer cracked his whip and tightened the reins. The horses broke into a gallop. The chariot jolted violently as it sped down the road, leaving the gaunt mob far behind.

Mazdad sat in the chariot, his face turned away. There were no tears in his eyes, only a burning sensation, as if a fire blazed behind his pupils. His mind raced with verses from the Avesta . . .

"*And those who cultivate the land with both arms, there are no beings more fortunate and blessed upon the face of the earth. May they be blessed, and may joy fill their dwelling places. Most venerable, most noble, most favored are they who sow the seeds, tend them, and bring in the harvest. Darkness and sorrow shall not enter their homes, which will be filled with the light of heaven. They are true to the covenant of Ahura Mazda's creation. And when the boughs of barley ripen, the color drains from Ahriman's face; when the grain reaches their dwellings, the malevolent spirits weep; and when the grain is ground into flour, darkness, evil, and Ahriman flee from their dwelling places—for grain and flour are their death. And these are the fortunate ones!*"

Mazdad recited in a harsh undertone. He looked upward. "Nay, O Lord of Earth and Heaven! O Lord of Paradise, Hell, and Purgatory! Your *Yazd* is losing, and Ahriman is winning. Darkness is prevailing. Evil is prevailing. And it is happening before our very eyes.

"*O righteous man of the Lord! Do not lust, do not rage. Each of you shall fill his belly only with the provisions he reaps with his toil, and shall consume it with moderation.*"

Mazdad was recalling the Avesta.

From his toil! His toil?

A mocking laugh rose within him.

"Today, there is such an abundance of grain in the capital that every citizen could eat his fill for a year. But where is it? Locked away in the godowns of nobles and mobeds. Most of it will likely rot, or be sold off to the Romans. They have never toiled a day in their lives. The nobles know nothing of labor. They swing one leg on top of the other, living lives of idle comfort. Their greatest concern is the royal hunt, and even that is carried out by the poor farmers and shepherds, who chase and corner the animals so the nobles can strike the final blow at their leisure and bask in the thrill of the kill.

"As for moderation? Their Roman companions are famed for their gluttony. They gorge themselves until their bellies are ready to burst, then they vomit to make room for more—only to resume partaking in the most delectable victuals. They are vile, but they are nobles. And even if they were to bathe night and day in the river itself, they would never be cleansed."

How did I become so callous? Mazdad wondered, a flicker of fear in his heart. He hadn't always been this cynical. Like a true Zoroastrian, he was of "good thoughts, good words, and good deeds," in accordance with Ahura Mazda's edict. But something had changed. It had begun on one of the early days of the famine, when he had been coming out of the fire temple. At the threshold, he ran into a distraught farmer. The man's face bore the unmistakable marks of starvation. In his arms he cradled a child who must have been three or four years old. He stood frozen, like a statue.

"What's wrong, farmer?" Mazdad asked.

"My child!" he cried. "My child hasn't eaten in days. Look what's happened." Mazdad gently pushed aside the tangle of hair from the child's delicate face and laid one hand on the forehead. The body was ice-cold, the shriveled, pink lips drooping lifelessly. The rows of dark lashes beneath closed eyes rested still against the child's cheeks. The child had died long ago.

"You're a healer! Heal him, kind master!" the farmer pleaded.

"Why didn't you come . . . to ask for grain sooner?" Mazdad asked, swallowing hard.

"You had already given away all the grain of the fire temple to the farmers," replied the farmer dejectedly. "I would have brought some from home . . ." Mazdad began, then halted mid-sentence. A pained expression crossed his face. It was impossible. How many mouths could he feed from his own stores? As it were, he never claimed a large portion for himself, only enough to feed his family. He wasn't one to hoard.

At last, he lifted his eyes and said quietly: "Farmer, your child is dead . . . he . . . he should be buried."

Zoroastrians did not lay out their children on a *dokhma*—or "Tower of Silence"—the round Parsi funerary tower of stone, where a corpse is laid out in order to be consumed by wandering scavengers, chiefly vultures. Nor could the poor afford proper funerary rites or offerings. Even the ritual purification of the body with consecrated bull's urine was far too expensive. Death was a costly affair. The poor often fell into debt just to afford it, ensnared for years in the cycle of loan repayment. For the elites, death was a grand occasion to put their wealth and rank on display. But a dirt-poor farmer? During a famine? Mazdad braced himself, expecting the farmer to break into sobs at any moment. In recent months, he had grown accustomed to the furor of lamentations, which rose frequently from poverty-stricken areas. But this farmer's response was unexpected. He stared wide-eyed at Mazdad, then laughed and said quietly:

"No, no, just look . . . he's alive . . . look."

He opened the child's eyes with his fingers to show Mazdad his catatonic brown pupils. Then he opened the child's mouth. He was overjoyed when he saw the rows of tiny, sparkling teeth.

"He's alive. He's alive! Look at him—he's just not moving."

At the sight of the starving father's wretched state, even the hard-hearted, lance-carrying guards of the fire temple couldn't help but feel moved. Their eyes welled with tears and they lowered their heads. Mazdad stood there, lips pressed tight. The child's corpse had to be taken care of. Would the farmer be able to bury it in his present mental state? Certainly not. And who else could touch the body? A dead body was impure. Once the soul departed, it left the body polluted—so much so that it soon began to reek. It could only be touched by the *nasusalars*—the corpse-bearers—and even they were required to undergo ritual bathing afterward to cleanse themselves of the contamination.

Mazdad looked from the dead child to his father, who was laughing and smiling vacantly. Overcome, Mazdad burst into sobs. He wept openly, his strong frame racked with hiccups. The guards stood frozen, unnerved to see their mobed in such a state. They didn't know what to do. In that moment, their hearts brimmed with a strange mix of reverence and tenderness for him. They had never liked Mazdad, but now, an unexpected sympathy rose within them.

Mazdad wept for a while, then fell silent. He gently extracted the child's corpse from the farmer's arms, and walked briskly toward the fields. The farmer hurriedly fell into step with him. "He will get better . . . just give him some medicine," he kept repeating. Around the fields lay mass graves of farmers who had died of starvation. A few other farmers milled around nearby. Mazdad laid the corpse gently on the ground. Tearfully, the farmers began to dig a fresh grave.

From that day on, Mazdad never shed a tear at the plaintive cries of a starving mob. Even now, as his chariot made its way toward his home, the memory flickered through his mind like a living photograph—fleeting, vivid, then gone. He drew in a deep breath and made a vow to himself: *I will act with wisdom and judgment. Wisdom is a virtue. To be swept away by emotion, to wail and scream—that is not wisdom. It is wickedness. Ahriman, you shall never triumph over me.*

CHAPTER 2

As Mazdad turned onto the pathway leading to his house, he noticed a bejeweled chariot parked in front of his garden walls. He recognized it immediately. "Seyavash!" he exclaimed happily. Seyavash was Mazdad's close friend. He was a noble commander of the King's army, and a dear friend to King Qobad. He held the title of "Hazar Pati"—Commander of a Thousand Men—and had one thousand warriors under his command. Seyavash enjoyed a deep closeness with Qobad. He was a pleasant-natured, sincere, and brave man. These qualities had won Qobad over. He would visit the palace without any restrictions, and often attended drinking parties with Qobad. He was also Qobad's partner in chess and polo. Once in a while, Qobad liked to see him alone. He trusted Seyavash. A friendship had developed between the young king and commander, founded on mutual admiration and trust.

The reason behind Mazdad's friendship with Seyavash was different. It so happened that Mazdad's father Bamdad and Seyavash's father both came from the small town of Madharaya, and had arrived at the kingdom around the same time. Their families knew each other. Their households used the same spices to prepare their meals. Their accents and jokes were similar. They used the same proverbs. In a kingdom full of diverse peoples, the kind of familiarity Seyavash enjoyed with Mazdad was unlike what he felt with anyone else. Both were of the same age, and appreciated the good human qualities in each other. They trusted one another. Sometimes, after supper, Seyavash would laugh and say:

"Say what you will, but proverbs are the bedrock of our friendship!"

Mazdad found Seyavash outside his great haveli. He was standing in the middle of the withered garden, hunched over the edge of the beautiful pond lined with rocks in hues of vermilion and azure. He held a broken branch in his hands and played with the colorful fish in the pond, sluggish and barely floating along in the little moss-covered water that was left.

Mazdad's face lit up when he saw Seyavash. Arms opened wide, he walked toward his friend: "Welcome, welcome!" Mazdad said happily. They embraced each other and chatted as they stepped into the house. The vast doors had been flung open. Inside, soft floor rugs were lined with bolster pillows. Decorative pots and vases adorned tables of different sizes. One corner was covered by a large carpet with a sizeable low table upon it. A chess board lay upon the table. In a lapis lazuli box were chess pieces carved out of black and white marble. A glazed blue tray filled with dry fruits rested on a little center table.

Seyavash and Mazdad sat down on the carpet, and began talking exuberantly.

"I have come to return Yaqutdokht," said Seyavash. "My bondmaid is back."

"Ah!" Mazdad acknowledged cheerfully. Yaqutdokht was not only Mazdad's bondmaid but also his *čagar* wife—a "dutiful wife" or "subordinate wife"—who, by custom, could be offered to friends and relatives for a short while when needed. Denag, by contrast, was the *padashah* wife—king-wife—a man's first and official wife. Bamdad had arranged the marriage in Mazdad's youth. Mazdad's mother had died in his early childhood, and Bamdad needed a lady of the house to manage household affairs. Bamdad never forgave himself, because his beautiful niece, who was now his daughter-in-law, soon fell gravely ill. Within a year, both her legs shriveled, and she could no longer walk. Lying in bed, she looked on with wistful, longing eyes. Gradually, she stopped speaking altogether.

Bamdad saw this as a terrible misfortune upon his household—a divine trial for which he and his son had proved themselves worthy. Mazdad didn't divorce Denag. He treated his ill, crippled wife with gentleness and compassion, often carrying trays of food to her bed with his own hands.

Though Mazdad had several *čagar* wives, Yaqutdokht was special. A farmer's daughter, she was an industrious, hardworking, and beautiful young woman. She was witty and intelligent, with a mellifluous voice. Mazdad's heart stirred with love and tenderness for this rural beauty. He often slept with her, or spent time with her in the garden as she watered the plants and sang sweet melodies. He felt a twinge of sorrow at parting from Yaqutdokht, but when Seyavash requested her for a few days—while his own bondmaid traveled to her village for childbirth—Mazdad could not refuse. He held Seyavash in no less regard than Yaqutdokht. After all, feelings of honor and jealousy had no place when it came to a customary ritual.

"Indeed! She'll be just right for you. She's the best," Mazdad said, giving Seyavash a pat on the shoulders.

"But, you . . ." Seyavash hesitated.

"No, my friend!" Mazdad replied. "She is not my property." Then, after a pause, he added pensively: "A woman is no one's property."

He looked closely at Seyavash, then turned his eyes toward the doorway. "Property! What a hollow word. What property? Have you seen the ruins of Jamshed's throne? Even that mighty castle is crumbling. The property endures . . . but the owner? Gone—like dry leaves in the wind."

Seyavash laughed.

He had always liked his friend's philosophical musings. They flowed like poetry—and what Persian heart did not cherish poetry? Seyavash happily took Yaqutdokht home with him. Mazdad missed her—especially at night—but soon after, the famine struck and every ounce of his being became consumed by starving farmers and their inevitable deaths. Still, when Yaqutdokht returned, he felt relief settle over him.

"Where is she?" he asked, delighted.

"In the harem," Seyavash replied. "She's serving Banu-e-Kadkhoda. I said *adaab* to them—and to your venerable father—before coming here." He tossed a few kernels of pistachios into his mouth. "Now, I'd like some of your special rose sherbet, the kind they make in Madharaya, and then I'll take my leave."

"No, no!" Mazdad replied. "How can you leave without having a meal? Let me have a *dastarkhwan* laid out for us." He clapped his hands sharply. A servant appeared, took the order, and departed.

"A meal! Gladly!" Seyavash smiled. "Nowhere in the entire city will I find food like that prepared in your home." He relished the meals at Mazdad's house, even though no meat was served. Mobeds were forbidden from partaking in meat. They were allowed to store no more than a year's worth of grain at their house, and only a year's worth of clothing. Mazdad was content with these restrictions. He neither had a taste for meat, nor any particular interest in clothes. Unlike those priests who kept their storehouses filled with grain and their havelis stacked with silks and brocades, Mazdad lived simply. Some might don plain cloaks in their fire-temples, but in the evenings they feasted at the palaces of the aristocracy, their glittering robes rivaling the splendor of any aristocratic attire.

Seyavash and Mazdad began to chat.

"How about a game of chess while we wait?" Mazdad suggested.

"Last time, you captured my king," Seyavash replied with a grin. "Today I'll even the score."

"The king!" Mazdad exclaimed suddenly. "Your king's days are numbered, Seyavash."

"Whatever do you mean?" Seyavash asked, alarmed. "What king?"

"The King of Kings—Qobad," Mazdad said solemnly. "The aristocracy and scribes have resolved to overthrow the crown."

"How do you know this?" Seyavash asked, his voice laced with concern.

"Last week, I traveled to the Farajam estate to perform wedding rites. After supper, a group of selected nobles gathered in the back garden. Several chief mobeds were there, along with some commanding officers. I, too, was invited to the gathering. This was the topic of their discussion."

"In your presence?"

"Nobody suspects me. I am a mobed, after all. As always, the aristocrats have the support of the clergy. The mobeds are mules, their reins tightly held by the nobility."

"And who do they want to crown king?" Seyavash asked quickly.

"Zarmeher . . ."

"Zarmeher!" Seyavash sucked in his breath. Zarmeher was a noble of the highest rank—a wicked, greedy man who flayed farmers alive on his countless estates. He plundered priceless silk brocades from shopkeepers and sold it in Rome and Arabia. His relentless coercion and insatiable greed were wreaking havoc on the Iranian silk trade.

Seyavash's heart ached for Qobad.

He was deep in thought, his forehead creased with worry—and rage.

"But . . . Zarmeher?" he whispered.

"They have even tracked down a boy from the Ashkanian dynasty. He's in Bakhtarayah—a child of fifteen or sixteen. They are conspiring to place him on the throne, with Zarmeher pulling the strings."

Seyavash cursed under his breath, grinding his teeth.

"Don't be like that, Seyavash!" Mazdad chided gently, placing a hand on his friend's shoulder. "Be sensible. Come, let's eat."

The food had been laid out on the *dastarkhwan*. Bamdad joined them and took a seat, ill at ease by the tension in the air.

Seyavash usually enjoyed dining at Mazdad's. Tonight, a special rustic *dehqani* meal had been prepared for him—vegetables soaked in pomegranate juice and cooked with spinach, vinegar, and flour. But no one seemed to enjoy the food today. Seyavash stopped eating.

"I should go now," he said. He bowed and offered *adaab* to Bamdad, who gave his blessings. As Seyavash turned to leave, he paused and looked back at Mazdad.

"We shall meet again soon, my friend. You'll be faithful to me, won't you?"

"Always. I am a devoted mobed."

Seyavash gave a faint smile.

"Indeed. But today, I almost wish you were a commander of an army . . . like me."

CHAPTER 3

Together with Yaqutdokht after many days—solitude and fragrance.

"How have you been?"

"I've been well."

"And Seyavash turned out to be . . . ?"

"Charming."

Mazdad turned on his side, propping himself up on his elbow. He laughed softly.

"Who told you to always speak the truth?"

"You did!"

"No. The truth is not required at this moment. Say something that will delight me . . ." Mazdad murmured, as his fingers gently caressed Yaqutdokht's brow and lips, as though painting them into existence.

"Are you not pleased?"

"I am pleased. Tonight, we'll make love like the Greeks."

Yaqutdokht smiled, her teeth sparkling like a string of pearls behind rosy lips.

But suddenly, the parted lips of the farmer's dead child flashed before Mazdad's eyes. He faltered. He saw starving farmers fall before him, one after another. He shut his eyes, but the image lingered. His advancing hands fell limply on the bed. For a few moments, he stared at the ceiling, silent.

"Not today," he said softly.

Yaqutdokht opened her mouth to speak, but thought better of it.

"All right," she said.

Mazdad slipped his feet into his shoes and stepped out of the room. Bamdad was standing against a pillar in the semi-circular veranda that curved around the bedrooms. His white garments and beard shone in the yellow moonlight.

"Where are you going at this hour, my child?" he asked, his old voice trembling.

"Nowhere, Baba," said Mazdad. "Just to the back garden."

With heavy steps, Bamdad headed toward his bedroom. A fear had begun to take root in his heart for his only son, Mazdad, the heir granted to him by Mazda. *Lord of Celestial Light, protect him*, he prayed, his eyes glistening. Mouthing supplications, he disappeared into his room.

CHAPTER 4

Mazdad's fire-temple was situated near the farmers' settlements on the outskirts of the city, with a number of estates stretching eastward. These settlements were home to miners, artisans, and ordinary shopkeepers—people who often left to establish new communities of their own, yet never abandoned their fire-temple. Even now, they came whenever they could to pay homage to their revered chief mobed. Here, they were never coerced into paying taxes. Here, they beheld Mazdad—the strange, quiet, melancholy sage whose eyes once shone with deep benevolence, but now flashed with a silent, ominous warning. From time to time, even the nobles of the neighboring estates came to the fire-temple to offer their respects.

CHAPTER 5

Mazdad ascended the stairs with measured steps and entered the fire-temple. A crowd of chiefs and lords awaited him. At his approach, they straightened and bowed. "Great mobed," they said respectfully, "we beg you—do not give the grain and silver of the offerings to the farmers today. It would be a sin, exalted one. These gifts are meant for you, and for us."

"We'll die of starvation."

"We'll starve!"

Their whispers snapped and hissed like snakes. Speechless, Mazdad walked on, head bowed in silence. He knew very well that the governors' granaries were brimming with grain. Yet instead of contentment at their stocks of victuals, restlessness and fear had taken hold of their hearts. *What if our provisions run out? How can we add to them still?*

He kept walking quietly. He did not wish to despise them. They were in the grip of the Foul Spirit; their greed and avarice were not their fault. Mazdad continued toward the pond.

I shall purify myself. My Lord, God of Clemency and Gladness, have mercy on me, he prayed softly.

At the fire-temple, mobeds were required to pray five times each day and night—a tradition dating back to the age before

Mazdakism, when Mithra was worshipped. Mithra, the Sun God, was revered by the inhabitants of Babylonia as celestial light and the source of the sacred fire. The prayer times followed the sun's course—the first at sunrise, the second when the sun was halfway from its zenith, the third as it began its descent, the fourth at sunset, and the fifth when daylight gave way to night.

"Purity and cleanness—cleanness and purity—these are righteousness," he recited from the Avesta.

Mazdad began the purification rite. As he recited the ordained prayers, he washed his hands up to the wrists three times, and splashed his face three times as well. Next, he rinsed his right hand and washed the right foot to the ankle three times, then repeated the process with his right hand and left foot. Finally, he washed both hands once more up to the wrists, and gently dried his hands and face with a towel.

He was ready to offer the litany to the fire.

He walked past unlit chambers scented with oud and frankincense. A priest stepped forward and covered Mazdad's nose with a strip of cloth, so his breath wouldn't pollute the fire. In a dark, octagonal chamber, the flames of the sacred fire blazed upon an altar. Glinting in their glow were metal apparatuses—curtain hooks, a mortar, tongs, and a crescent-shaped table upon which lay twigs from the hallowed barsom tree. Mazdad began chanting prayers from the holy book in their prescribed order and number, his voice rising and falling like the cadences of an anthem. With engraved silver tongs, Mazdad threw purified kindling upon the flames. He then poured an offering of the consecrated hom plant into the fire. Next, the *zaotar*, or the officiating priest, intoned the prescribed invocations in their sacred order. Seven priests stood attentively beside the *zaotar*, serving as his assistants. The first was the *hāwanān*, who pounded the hom plant in the mortar. Second came the *ākhrosh*, keeper of the sacred fire, who at times lent his voice to the *zaotar*'s chant. The third was the *frābaretar*, tasked with bringing the kindling wood. Fourth stood the *āberat*, or water bearer. Fifth was the *āsnātar*, who washed the hom. Sixth came the *raethwishkara*, who mixed hom with milk. The seventh and final priest was the *sraoshavarez*, or the master of rituals, who enforced discipline and obedience, and oversaw the training of new initiates.

What a big fuss, Mazdad often thought. Fire-temples seemed to be sprouting in every corner of the city. *I could have performed all these duties myself.* He would smirk at the thought. To him, these fire-temples had become little more than sources of income for the mobeds and their sycophants. That in itself might have been tolerable, but for each ritual, the mobeds and lords alike coerced the poor into giving offerings. Intimidation and greed had seeped into their natures. Here, in the fire-temple, their attention was not on the sacred fire, but on the offerings brought by the supplicants. *What is the use of so many fire-temples?* he thought bitterly. *Their overabundance has turned the sacred fire into a mockery.*

A group of frightened farmers stood at the entranceway. The chiaroscuro of light and dark in the fire-temple struck them with awe and wonder. In that shifting veil between light and darkness, a divine mystery seemed to dwell, and their hearts trembled before it. To them, it was the splendor of Ahura Mazda made visible, with the power to relieve all their sorrows.

"They wish to speak with me," Mazdad said to the lords.

"Supreme mobed," the hom pounder said quietly, "there is not a single grain left in the granaries. All has already been divided between you and us, according to our shares."

"What business is that of yours?" Mazdad snapped. "Return to your posts—all of you."

The lords hurried out. The starving farmers looked on in awe. They longed to speak, to beg the mobed to pray for them, to call upon the Almighty to soften the nobles' hearts, that they might show mercy and offer some charity. But Mazdad gave them no chance. His eyes quickly swept the room; then, without a word, he thrust the pair of silver tongs into the tattered robes of the nearest farmer.

"Smelt it, then sell it," he whispered. "Share the proceeds equally. Be warned! Now go." With that, he turned and left the room.

The farmers stood dumbstruck. *No, no!* they longed to refuse. Their hearts quivered at the thought of leaving with the sacral tongs of the fire-temple. But another fire burned deep in their bellies. Was this fire sacred, or was it polluted? The fire in their bellies that gnawed at their lives and their family's lives with every passing moment. They were under great duress. This was not theft—the great mobed himself had placed the tongs in their hands. It was a gift from Ahura Mazda, his benediction. The farmer gripped the tongs tightly under his arm. In moments, they were gone.

When the time came for the afternoon prayer, a commotion rose within the fire-temple.

"Where are the silver tongs? The sacred, priceless silver tongs!"

"It seems someone has taken them," Mazdad said carelessly. "Fetch another pair from the storehouse—we have plenty."

"Thievery—in a house of worship!" the lords hissed through clenched teeth beneath the high pillars of the fire-temple. "This is the result of indulging the farmers! They had 'thief' written all over their faces! Alas, our mobed will be our undoing!"

CHAPTER 6

Exactly three days later, some shocking news shook this starving town: Zarmeher had been murdered on his estate. Seven army generals had come to dine at his house. At some point, a quarrel erupted. The guards reported seeing riders galloping away in haste. Inside, they found Zarmeher's decapitated body, drenched in blood.

Among the nobility, Shapur Mehran's name was being whispered in suspicion. But the rumors soon came to an abrupt halt. No one had the nerve to carry the conversation forward. Shapur Mehran was a general, the commander-in-chief of the king's army. Did this mean he was loyal to Qobad? That remained to be seen. For now, silence seemed to be the wisest course. On this, the nobles, landlords, and scribes were all in agreement. Few attended Zarmeher's final rites. Only his family was present. First off, he was dead, so what was the point? Second, his death was plainly an act of persecution. That much was clear.

Seyavash met Mazdad outside the fire-temple, dressed in his army uniform, the gold-plated chains of his livery catching the sun.

"Your people have claimed a life," Mazdad said in a low voice. "His soul will wander for all eternity."

"That is what his soul deserves," Seyavash replied curtly. "What did you expect—that the entire Iranian empire fall prey to that power-hungry wretch?"

"It is a sin," Mazdad said. "Intimidation would have sufficed."

"Impossible," Seyavash shot back. "He would have finished us off. And God forbid, his first scheme was to have the King murdered. Aren't you loyal to the King?"

"I admire the King, Seyavash. He is a just, kind-hearted, and fair-minded young man."

"I know," Seyavash said with a smile. Then, lowering his voice, he added, "I want you to meet him. It shall be arranged in a few days." He spurred his horse and sped away. Mazdad watched him disappear into the winding pathways.

Sometimes, he thought, *I feel that if Seyavash's horse had wings, it would take flight.*

CHAPTER 7

Mazdad among the anxious farmers.

"I gave a handful of grain to each of you. That is all that arrived at the fire-temple today. Yet you know the nobles' warehouses are full."

Silence. Dark, disappointed eyes darting within sunken sockets.

"My brothers! This world—its earth, its water—was created by the great Almighty. How, then, can it belong to any one man? You are the ones who labor upon it in the summer and winter. You sow seeds, and bring in the harvest—it is yours. The grain belongs to the hands that tend to it and bring it to life. It is you who fulfill the will of the supreme and magnificent Ahura Mazda, making the earth flourish with crops, fruits, and flowers. The nobles and scribes are nothing but robbers. Why not take back what's rightfully yours?"

"That cannot be, lord. It's impossible!"

"They'll trample us beneath their horses' hoofs."

"Or the cavalry might become your ally," Mazdad replied. "They too are scraping by on meager incomes—and they know you. When the King goes to war, who are the foot soldiers marching behind his army? You are those soldiers. He owes his victories to you."

Silence . . .

"The aristocrats have their own private armies, and what you are suggesting—it's a sin! That's not what the noble Prophet preached. We'll be disgraced in both worlds, great mobed!"

Hunger pervaded the city. It had hit the craftsmen the hardest, whose skills were famed across the sultanate of Rum, so much so that they had begun to imitate them. Food had become so costly that merchants and traders were forced to spend their entire incomes on rations. They could no longer afford the work of artisans, and their families edged closer to starvation.

And then there were laborers, who mined gold, silver, iron, lead, and salt. One of them was Panah Barzin—hefty and dark, with large, blistered hands, his hair and eyelashes crusted with salt.

"Bathe yourself!" Mazdad warned. "Or you will dissolve whole, like salted meat."

"There's no water. They've taxed it," Barzin said, looking at Mazdad with wide, dark eyes. "I keep licking salt, and it makes me want to vomit."

"This is a system built on injustice," said Mazdad.

"That's right!"

"There is plenty of grain in the city. We should break the locks on the warehouses and take it."

"Yes!"

"Then why don't you?"

"I will. A few of us have decided—tonight, we're breaking into one of the warehouses."

"What?" Mazdad shifted uneasily. "You're going to steal? That is a sin."

"Beloved lord, whatever do you mean?"

"Don't do it under the cover of night, but in broad daylight—demand what's yours, and take it. Panah Barzin, will you take me to the laborers?"

"I will."

Mazdad met with the laborers—miners, shepherds, woodcutters, and masons. They fell at his feet, weeping. To them, there was no way out but theft and robbery. And when they got caught, they were tortured to death. What Mazdad was preaching had never been done before. They could not even picture it—equal share in everything? Impossible! Their last words were always the same: "But that is not what the Great Messenger taught. This will be a kingdom of sin."

But the laborers and farmers of the region had begun to revere Mazdad. They never prostrated themselves before him—he would chide them, saying: "I am a human like you." Yet they could not find words for the love they bore him. In times of famine, mobs of hungry laborers flocked around him. It was then he was named *Mazdak*—a name soon to be renowned throughout the Sasanian Empire.

Then there were the scribes—scholarly and well-groomed men who sat in long, rectangular rooms, surrounded by reams of parchment, transcribing every imaginable subject in a flowing calligraphic hand. Their never-ending task was to translate Avestan texts from their archaic tongue into the modern Pahlavi, inscribing them in the new script that Mani had introduced to the kingdom. They were also responsible for recording royal and official edicts, transcribing civil court rulings, and compiling poetry collections and the writings of the King's poets, which later came to be known as *divans*. The tradition of composing *divans* had made a poet out of many a scribe—and they loathed one another even more than they hated the nobles. Skilled men across the kingdom had their unions, but the scribes could never come together. Each saw the other as his fiercest rival. But the famine had weakened their constitution as well. Their wages had dwindled while the price of provisions soared. Word of a new name was spreading—*Mazdak*. But who was Mazdak? What was he preaching? Would they be asked to transcribe his speeches? They caught whispers of such rumors now and then. And why not—so long as it brought no persecution and earned them some remuneration. They would string words together like rows of fine pearls. Shared rights? The idea wasn't half-bad. None of them enjoyed any special privileges, and such a change might well work to their advantage.

And then there was Borzuya, the royal physician—a disciple of Jalinus—who had journeyed through Rum, the land of Hind, and Arabia. In all the realm, no master of Greek medicine surpassed his learning.

"What do you say?" his patients would ask.

"I prefer to listen," Borzuya would reply. He was quite a wealthy man, a surgeon who had saved lives and healed nobles. His private lands, small palace, and wealth were the fruits of his skill, tireless labor, and professional devotion.

"Meaning, which system?" people would inquire.

He would enumerate the ingredients of a prescription, then add, "Crush and strain these, and drink with warm water. Your cold will be cured. As for the system, this is what it was, is, and will remain so."

"But, my lord?" his beloved Banu-e-Quz asked. "The farmers' kin who work for daily wages in our house are dying of strange new illnesses, the likes of which I have never seen. I am weary of so much death. What are these diseases, and what cures them?"

“The cure for hunger is food. As a devout Zoroastrian, I give in charity. And these days, I give more than ever.”

“But . . .”

“But I haven’t enough grain to feed thousands every day. Tell me truly, my beautiful—are all people really equal? Are other physicians my equals? By no means. In the name of equality, novices will steal my prescriptions and botch the formulas. The study of medicine itself will deteriorate. Mazdak is prescribing a recipe for disaster.”

Mazdak consulted with many mobeds.

Priests from both humble shrines and grand fire-temples held Mazdak in high regard for his competence, integrity, and strict moral code. But his unorthodox vision troubled them.

“Exalted mobed, it is true that the serfs and farmers are surviving in wretched conditions, but contentment . . .”

“Contentment, my gracious friends?” Mazdak broke in. “Telling the nobles to be content with their palaces, their thousands of slaves and bondmaids, their wives, their fine foods, their overflowing granaries and stables, and telling a starving serf in rags to be content, are these the same thing? Impossible! True contentment can only exist when everyone has the means to fulfill their most basic needs, so that none must steal, and none fall prey to base desires. That is the spirit of the word. Are we not, then, misconstruing the meaning of the holy book?”

“Honorable mobed, the Foul Spirit and the All-good Spirit have been at war since the dawn of creation. In the end, the All-good Spirit will prevail.”

“But how will it prevail? That victory is only possible through us.”

“Ahriman has ruled the living world for nine thousand years.”

"Those nine thousand years have passed. Should we not rise now and join forces with the All-good Spirit, to secure its supremacy?"

"Your Reverence," they replied, "goodness will win its freedom from darkness, as it was once overcome. Our duty is to strive for that freedom through pure thoughts, pure deeds, and pure words."

"To be pure in deed means that, in this war between good and evil, we ourselves must triumph over evil."

These debates usually ended without resolution. Yet Mazdak's words had begun to take root in the hearts of certain mobeds. These words came from a man whose virtue was beyond question. It was startling how the words spoken or written by a single person could take hold of another's heart like that, as if cast by a spell. Words—shaped from sound. "Aa," "ba," "pa," "ta," brought into being by the miraculous faculty of the human tongue. Sounds fused to form meaning—meaning that became thoughts. More than thoughts. And these thoughts, finer than ether, emerged from a mere lump of flesh. Within the mouth, teeth, palate, and lips joined to utter: "Almighty lord, venerated saint! Then is all matter truly polluted?"

Mazdak spoke of such matters to others as well, yet only the Sufis listened with rapt attention.

In their vast shrine, he sat with his legs folded beneath him on an embroidered felt rug laid over the checkered black-and-white marble floor. Before him sat a Zoroastrian Sufi, lips curled in a faint smile, his face aglow, half-open eyes were fixed on some faraway grove of lush trees. From time to time, he murmured words of wonder.

"The sounds that are formed in our mouths . . ." Mazdak began, voicing his private thoughts.

"Indeed!" the Sufi replied. "Extraordinary." He concentrated on Mazdak, and added: "And faces—are they not extraordinary as well? Look at this long torso, and the face poised upon it—ears, eyes, nose—absorbing and imbibing the universe each moment. And among them, the mouth . . . ah, the mouth is most remarkable. Lips, palate, gullet, teeth, tongue—the passageway through which we absorb nourishment. The lips grant us the pleasure of taste, and when they meet another's lips, that pleasure stirs to life. Yet of all these, the tongue is most fascinating. The tongue—that conjures the very sensation of taste. Ah! What is this mystery?" The Sufi began to sway. "Sweet, bland, bitter, salty . . . what are they? Why are they?" he seized Mazdak's hand.

The Sufi leaned forward and raised a finger, as if unveiling a profound secret.

"These are hidden everywhere, yet remain unseen. They only manifest when the tongue awakens them. They cannot be seen or heard, though they may be smelled. Only in union with the tongue do they reveal their secrets and full majesty of their being. And the tongue, housed within our mouth, works with the teeth, palate, and lips to shape sounds into letters, letters into words, words into names. The names of all things! Such marvels dwell within our mouth," he said, his eyes alight with wonder as he looked upon Mazdak.

"The human mouth contains the entire universe," said Mazdak.

"Wondrous . . . wondrous . . ." the Sufi murmured. Then, he lost himself in his thoughts and began to sing in a slow, trance-like voice:

O sweetness,
O saltiness—
From what veiled realm do you come?

To us earthly children, you come—
A guest, ever-changing,
Quiet within your hidden shell.
Bitterness becomes sweetness,
What mystery do you conceal?
Only the tongue may know—
Only the tongue.

"Indeed!" Mazdak whispered. Rising to his feet, he walked toward the doorway of the shrine just as a troupe of musicians entered, carrying their instruments. That evening, the troupe was performing at a gathering of song and dance. The lord's disciples would serve as attendants of "ecstasy" in Ahura Mazda's court. Tonight was a Sufi mystic's night of ecstasy, and a ceremony had been planned. It was a night cloaked in mystery. The outside world knew little of it, their knowledge confined to frivolous rumors drifting outside the walls of the shrine.

Mazdak had not received a direct answer from the Sufi, yet his own ideas had been affirmed. He smiled, finding it endearing when someone strove to get to the heart of every matter. *They are empiricists*, he thought, *never closing the door to curiosity and inquiry*. They pondered over each part of the human body. They would marvel at the male organ, exclaiming: "Wondrous! Wondrous!" What was this, if not an instrument for Zoran—the divine force of our boundless universe—to execute his intentions? And wasn't its vigor a manifestation of creation's own ecstasy? Dormant in slumber, it was roused and quickened by a mere touch.

For them, the male organ was the custodian of nature's forces, a sign of man's divine essence, honored and revered by all. They even considered it a privilege to adorn their turbans with its likeness, fashioned from velvet and filled with cotton.

With passing thoughts for the Sufis' way of life, Mazdak stepped outside and summoned his charioteer. His mind was once more preoccupied with letters.

Letters hold mystery; they carry power, he reflected as he climbed into the chariot.

CHAPTER 8

Joshwa the Jew came to see him after many days. He lived in the eastern region of Ctesiphon on a Jewish settlement that stretched far into the distance. The well-to-do there had weathered the famine without any hardship, but the poor Jews were reduced to begging for morsels of food.

Joshwa was a schoolteacher in his community. A middle-aged, handsome scholar, intent on gathering information about Zoroastrianism. That was why he had sought out Mazdak. On the surface, the two men could not have been more different—in their eating habits, their clothing, their family backgrounds—but despite their differences, some unspoken kinship had developed quickly between them. A kinship born of compassion, one that left both in a state of perpetual restlessness.

"Mobed," he said to Mazdak, "More than a thousand years ago my people, too, were given a dream—a vision of the Kingdom of God, where peace and contentment would reign, where the mighty would not torment the weak, and wolves would not rend lambs. We were told that a day would surely come when such a kingdom would be established."

"For thousands of years, mankind has yearned—across every land, every corner of the earth. The longing for peace and justice is much older than war and oppression . . . or perhaps they were born together. Why, in faraway corners of the world, has humanity clung to the belief that such a kingdom will one day be established? Because it is his need, and hence his desire." Mazdak paused. "I feel reassured after listening to you, Joshwa. But tell me—did your rabbis never think of the Jews who live in poverty and under oppression?"

"The Holy Torah strictly forbids the taking of exploitative interest," said Joshwa.

"Yet it is your people who collect compound interest on the loans aristocrats and mobeds give the poor, reaping lavish favors and gifts, and enforcing this system on a grand scale across the sultanate of Rum."

"Could they have accomplished anything without the cracking whips of the Rum and Persian armies behind them, Mazdak? We have been stateless for centuries. Exiles . . . yes, but exiles who are experts."

"And it was they who taught the Aryans to generate wealth from wealth?" Mazdak asked, his eyebrows arched. "I hear such dealings are common in the land of Hind as well."

"Wealth must multiply; otherwise, why would grand empires ever be established?"

"Hazrat Isa (Peace Be Upon Him)—or Yesu, the prophet of Jerusalem—lived among paupers. He taught that the poor are the salt of the earth, the fisherman and laborers who toil in its depths. He also foretold that a kingdom of justice would come, and that the poor shall inherit God's earth."

"Yesu!" exclaimed Joshwa.

"Prophet Yesu," Mazdak corrected.

Joshwa smiled, embarrassed. "We Jews do not regard him as a prophet."

"But why?" Mazdak asked, genuinely curious.

"He did not display the signs foretold in our holy book about the coming of the Prophet," said Joshwa.

"What signs?"

"First, the true prophet would rebuild Solomon's Temple. Isa did not."

Mazdak laughed. "He's discredited over such a small matter?" he said, then added with a mischievous glint in his eyes: "Or was the real reason that Yesu sought to preserve the purity of faith by purging it of the lust and greed of usury? He overturned the tables of the moneylenders in the temple."

"An unattainable desire," Joshwa remarked. "Without riches, my friend, what becomes of the pomp and splendor of temples, the awe and majesty of the mobeds?"

"But he was surely a prophet of God—the Lord spoke to him directly," said Mazdak. "He was a healer, like Mani. You know, Joshwa, Mani learned love, compassion, and forgiveness from Yesu's teachings. Yesu was the Messiah, and his hands possessed healing."

Mazdak could never speak such words to one of his own. His veneration for Mani was a secret he kept hidden in his heart.

Joshwa said: "I, too, am fond of Yesu, Mazdak . . . but that does not compel me to believe he is God. And then . . ."

"What?" Mazdak asked with interest.

"These Christians . . . look at them. The Nestorians and the Jacobites are at each other's throats, thirsty for blood over whether Yesu was of a singular nature or two—whether purely divine, or both human and divine. Even here, in Ctesiphon, the madrasas of the Christian settlements are constantly at odds with one another."

"Hm!" said Mazdak. He looked seriously at Joshwa. "The real quarrel was sown by their own leaders, fueled by the estates and lavish gifts the aristocracy and mobeds grant in exchange for their loyalty."

"Why? Don't thoughts and beliefs collide?"

"Thoughts?" Mazdak laughed. "They do, but thoughts alone do not spill blood. Blood is spilled by weapons—and weapons come from wealth. The wealthy invest their wealth for their own gain, my Jewish friend. Thoughts are *Yazd*; when they meet, they can unite, and then . . ."

"And then?" Joshwa repeated.

"A new thought is born," Mazdak declared with triumph. "Blessings! Blessings! Blessings upon the newborn! All people rejoice in celebration."

"And your own thoughts—whose did they unite with to come into existence?" asked the wise Jew.

Mazdak lowered his head, lost in thought. Then he looked up and said, "I cannot say for certain. Perhaps they were born when the longings of humankind converged. Joshwa, in my faith, all that exists in this world is a mere possibility. Yet 'goodness' is Ahura Mazda's intention, and its fulfillment has been entrusted to mankind. Man is Ahura Mazda's ally on earth."

They moved to an octagonal room for supper. Mazdak performed the necessary rites before sharing a meal with someone who was not of the same faith.

He frequently visited with Jews and Christians. The presence of Jews had spread far and wide across the provinces of Iran. Centuries ago, when Nebuchadnezzar exiled them from Jerusalem to Babel, and the region later fell under Sasanian rule following a war, these migrants not only settled within the Sasanian kingdom but also spread to distant cities and villages across the empire. Under Sasanian protection, their religious scholars completed the transcription of their sacred texts. At the same time, the foundational tenets of the Zoroastrian faith—belief in one God, the Day of Judgment, resurrection, paradise, and hell—were established in their book. Angels unfurled their pure wings and took flight in the people's imagination.

But the Iranian Christians were not migrants; they were the indigenous people of Iran, among the oldest Christians. Living at the crossroads of the Aramaean and Hebrew traditions, they were not devout Zoroastrians. Zoroastrianism had arrived here gradually, and in an ambiguous state at that. A thousand years before the birth of Hazrat Isa (PBUH), the First Prophet arrived in northern Iran, to the region of Bakhtarayah, or perhaps to Sistan, though who can say for certain? When Yesu's companion Tomas passed through these regions, many pledged their allegiance to him. Leaning on his staff, Tomas journeyed farther and farther into the distance. Some claimed he traveled southward and, like many others before him, vanished into the shadows of Hind. Meanwhile, Christians continued to spread across the far reaches of the empire. The Christian community in Ctesiphon was well-organized. And then . . . how strange! At the very border of the Sasanian empire, the Christian kingdom of Rum emerged. People rejoiced, and some even migrated to King Constantine's new empire. Most, however, stayed behind, though it was hardly surprising that their hearts were in Rum.

The Hebrews were tormented at the sight. The people of Rum had once overpowered and oppressed them, and now, instead of embracing the true faith, they had converted to Christianity. As Christians, they were now dominating and persecuting the Jews more than ever before.

Then, in the eastern quarter of Ctesiphon, there was a Sufi monastery nestled in a lush, verdant area. It served as a gathering place for Sufis. Once in a while, Mazdak visited as well, for no one was prohibited from visiting the monastery. Mazdak found it intriguing that people from every nation and faith gathered there, each claiming a bond with the Beloved. Among them were Hebrews, bringing with them their Qabalah philosophy; Christians who swayed with elation, and Zoroastrians too. None took issue with the others. They hewed to an all-encompassing conception of unity. Some claimed, "We are privy to the secret of the Beloved," while others, more blissfully, proclaimed, "We know not the secret of the Beloved—it lies beyond the orbit of human comprehension." What was extraordinary was that neither those who claimed to know nor those who claimed not to know did not get caught up in disputes or altercations. "Verily, those who do not know are the ones who know All," they conversed in obscure, esoteric riddles. The Sufis were deeply attuned to all that lay within the orbit of earthly knowledge. Hebrews pondered over alchemy, and Christians joined them. They conducted various alchemical experiments, mixing mysterious substances over fire to create different amalgams. All these experiments were kept secret, and outsiders speculated that they were searching for a formula to make gold. But Mazdak did not believe this. These were serious alchemists, dedicated to advancing Greek philosophy.

The eternally euphoric gathering was moved to tears by the famine, but not for their own sake. While practicing their spiritual exertions, they would fast for forty days at a time, standing on one leg for days on end, pushing their limits and subjecting their bodies to various forms of suffering in order to surrender their *nafs*—their ego—to the divine spirit. But they understood the difference between fasting and starving. Why does a man not perish after fasting for several days, whereas his body succumbs to starvation in such a short span of time? That, too, was a mystery. Fasting was an act of intention. It was the Sufi's intention that sustained him, while starvation was unintentional.

No, they wept for others. To their minds, the only solution was to evoke compassion among the nobles and aristocrats.

"Non-believers are not eligible to receive food in charity, for provisions are sacred" Mazdak said sympathetically to Joshwa. Then, he added, "This is yet another hypocrisy of the mobeds. What will one do with one's clothing and shoes if one is starving? I'll have to think of something else. Don't forget—it cannot be divine will that your dirt-poor, laboring people die in the agony of hunger pangs." Joshwa left.

Mazdak lay on his back upon the withered grass of the garden. The second half of the night was coming to an end. The air had cooled, and a pleasant breeze drifted in, carrying the faint scent of fragrant incense burning nearby. The Milky Way shimmered against an ink-blue sky. To soothe his eyes, Mazdak gazed intently at the galaxy. His people called it the "Path of the Cows." They revered cows and bulls. From Bakhtarayah to Ctesiphon, these animals had been the guarantors of his people's lives. The pure, milk-giving cow and bull had lived alongside them through the ages. Divine cosmic forces had not created Gayomars alone. Gayomars was born upon lofty mountains, alongside a white, immensely powerful bull. His real name was "Gayomartan"—"gayo," meaning mortal, and "martan," meaning blessed with life—mortal life. The bull was his companion, confronting the physical forces of nature head-on with his sharp, dagger-like, mighty horns. Like mortal beings, it was beautiful and majestic. Though it was neither obedient nor pure in nature like its female companion born later, it could be tamed. Riding upon the bull's back, Gayomars descended from the mountain's steep, stony heights.

For thousands of years, the Aryans were immersed in these thoughts.

Then, much happened.

On the fertile, green coast of Hind, Gautam arrived—an extraordinary mortal man who found a way out of suffering. He rejected the extremely rigid division of caste and race, which was said to have been introduced during Emperor Jamshed's reign, who lived so long ago that only forgotten stories remained of him. In Hind, Buddha welcomed into his monasteries those laboring castes whom the Hindu priests had deemed so impure that even to touch them—indeed, even for their shadow to fall upon another—was considered a grave sin. But even Buddha could not find a way out of poverty. None of the eight petals of his beautiful lotus flower pointed toward a path for change. "Obey the law," he had ordained. But what law? Exploiting poor farmers for forced labor was also considered a law. Then, Sekander came from Macedonia. His army defeated Dara, ruler of Arya—a strange king who was always accompanied by a flock of historians. He rode at full gallop along the vast highways built by the Sasanid kings, availing himself of the ample facilities for rest and sustenance in the spacious caravanserais constructed by those same kings, before going on to defeat the Aryans. His army razed all the fire-temples to the ground and burned the copies of the Avesta. These were the earliest Avestan manuscripts, inscribed on fine parchment made from vellum, when man had yet to learn the art of making paper.

"All this is false," declared Sekander. "I shall conquer the world to liberate it from tyranny and oppression." He believed only his way to be virtuous. Perhaps he took pride in his teacher . . . perhaps his teacher was worthy of such pride. Mazdak, lost in thought, reflected: *Aristotle was not a prophet, even though there was not a single worldly subject he had not yet pondered.*

Sekander left, taking his cavalry with him. A handful of people remained, holding on to Macedonian ideals—the five elements (clay, water, air, fire, ether), dialectics, and the tradition of discourse, for the Aryans argued over everything.

But weren't many of these ideals inspired by the Aryans? The famous ten thousand men who founded the civilization that would one day be known as the Greeks were, in fact, men assembled by Kourosh, the first Aryan king. They organized themselves as an army and settled in Iran, but when Kourosh surrendered his soul to his Maker, those ten thousand men—seeds of the Greek nation—set out on foot, eventually reaching Greece, where they at last found rest.

The Aryans did not understand ether; it was a Greek addition to the natural elements. Mazdak recalled that Mani's conception of "ether" as the essence of the universe had been inspired by the Greeks, who believed that at every moment, people all over the earth were in a constant state of give and take, with thoughts transferring swiftly from one mind to another.

But in this same Greece, this philosophers' paradise, poor Greeks were forced to sell themselves to pay off their debts. Rum followed the same custom. Each prosperous Greek owned at least one slave—someone who had been driven to sell himself or his son due to poverty. Several laws had been introduced regarding slavery—when it was permissible to beat a slave, and with what intensity; whether blood could be drawn or not; which parts of the body could be struck—Mazdak bit his lips bitterly.

A benevolent expression returned to his countenance when he remembered that Greek philosophy was exemplary. It had revived the Aryan concept of dialectical argument, which the Great Messenger Ahura Mazda confirmed through the opposition between light and darkness. The Greeks must have been Mazda's disciples. Zeus was the name they gave to Mazda, as they could not turn their tongues to pronounce the name correctly. Later, they returned to Iran.

The All-good Spirit was abundant and wholesome, while the Foul Spirit stood in opposition—an eternal battle!

A devout mobed who offered the five prescribed daily prayers in his fire-temple, Mazdak concluded his prayers with these words:

"O Ahura Mazda, we are your apprentices, and we seek to fulfill your intention. Grant us your favor, and we shall drive injustice from your land."

He repeated the prayer and closed his eyes. In that moment, he perceived a miracle—a miracle akin to Creation itself, revealed to a human being by a mysterious, utterly unknown force—an irrefutable and sublime miracle. Mazdak felt divine inspiration unfold its wings within his soul. He saw the sign clearly—so vast were the wings they spanned the whole sky. Immaculate, luminous, and whiter than milk, the wings shimmered with hues of blue and pink. They were strong, their feathers bound tightly like those of a pigeon. Mazdak saw the undersides of the wings clearly.

"If people can act only by the command of Ahura Mazda, then you are my Messenger," Mazdak heard distinctly.

His body was seized by tremors, as though snow were falling all around him and he were shivering from intense cold. Not only his body, but his very breath was trembling, and within his chest, his heart was beating very slowly. Mazdak opened his eyes. He could see the sky once more. The stars were shining. He was still trembling from head to toe. He gripped the dried grass tightly in his fists. He said:

"God is light. The elements of this light . . ."—Mani's words came back to him—"ether, air, light, water, and fire." Mazdak said firmly: "Matter! This earth? It is a sign of the All-good Spirit. The earth, too, is light."

He began again: "Light has three elements: water, fire, and earth. And in its presence dwell four powers: etiquette, reason, memory, and . . . joy. These four divine powers all dwell within human beings."

"And now, I must go in," he murmured under his breath. He stood up and went inside the house, to his fire-temple. "May this sacred fire remain lit forever," he said with a bowed head, and added a few more pieces of fragrant wood to the flames.

He walked toward his bedroom. A lamp was burning in Denag's chamber. He peeked into the room. Denag was still awake. "You're still awake? Go to sleep, my innocent king-wife," Mazdak said with tenderness and affection. He gently laid his hand upon Denag's forehead. Denag closed her eyes. Mazdak returned to his own chamber. Resolute and solemn, he stretched out upon his bed and fell asleep reciting prayers from the Avesta.

CHAPTER 9

Qobad entered his private chamber in the palace. He glanced around before reclining on his jeweled armchair. With a silk handkerchief, he wiped beads of perspiration off from his forehead, attempting to control the subtle tremors in his body. Then, he clapped. The gold-embroidered curtain shifted.

"Your majesty," said his chief maidservant from behind the curtain.

"Something to drink . . ." said Qobad. "Not alcohol—I've already had supper—water, or juice." A maidservant appeared with a crystal goblet on a gold tray, accompanied by a small dish of gold-covered pistachio kernels.

The maidservant disappeared.

Qobad sipped the cold juice, then fixed his eyes on the engravings on the wall.

He had just returned from a banquet with the city's prominent nobles, and was stunned by their impertinence. They had opposed every proposition he made without hesitation, turning to Jamasp each time they needed support. Jamasp, his younger brother, was still at a tender age. He was inexperienced, and not very wise. While he certainly enjoyed the sense of importance that came with being next to Qobad, he was unfamiliar with the affairs of state, and could only nod in agreement. The high-ranking officials, with cunning intent, made it seem as though Jamasp was in favor of their cause. "Precisely! His Highness is most discerning," they would repeat.

So, now they are luring Jamasp into their trap! Qobad thought, his thoughts darkening. *They want to crown him king. Well, they'll have to kill me first.*

Suddenly, he felt a wave of calm. He was a young man with nerves of steel, though he had yet to face a true test of his resolve. Perhaps the time had come.

How had he come by his crown and throne? If the White Huns had not defeated Shahanshah Peroz, it might never have been possible. They had attacked Iran before, but Bahram V and Yazdegerd II had driven them out. Then, Peroz became king—and he didn't last against the Hun army. It was a catastrophic defeat for the Persian empire. The king was compromised, and the aristocrats, nobles, and priests rose to power. Their influence continued to grow until the king was nothing more than a puppet in their hands.

Peroz fought bravely. He died on the battlefield while the White Huns were marching on Herat. It was the aristocrats who had put Peroz's paternal cousin on the throne. He was known as Balash. Or maybe it was Balach—with a *ch* sound, as in "chew"—a scion of the Sasanid family that had conquered the last province to the southeast of the kingdom: Makran, or Sistan. They had been living there for centuries. Political necessities had drawn notable individuals from all over the kingdom to the throne, but the Arabic pronunciation prevailed in Ctesiphon, and so, he came to be known as Balash. Balash was a kind and just king. Naturally, the aristocrats did not tolerate him for long. They had developed a taste for power and wealth. Knowing full well that Iran could not endure any more bloodshed, Balash sought peace with the White Huns. Years of war had already devastated the kingdom. The aristocrats, however, orchestrated a plot against him, blinding him by pouring molten lead in his eyes. It was then that they set their sights on Qobad, Balash's nephew. *Why? Because he was young, and they could make him their puppet?*

"But they were wrong," said Qobad. He was calm. He rose from the armchair, standing to his full height, and glanced at his turban, studded with genuine pearls. It sat on the alcove he had placed it on as he had entered the room. Then, he began pacing.

They were wrong, he thought again. The royal blood coursing through his veins carried a history that stretched back thousands of years. When he looked back at his past, he saw a constellation of figures—there was Ardeshir Babakan, who conquered Kirman, Isfahan, Fars, Susiyan, Bahrain, Sistan, Khurasan, and Margiana, who founded great cities like Ctesiphon and shaped the empire according to the Avesta; then, there was Shapur, who harnessed the waters of the oceans to build dams, under whose reign Aryan artwork flourished and reached as far as Khotan; and then, there were also Yazdegerd and Hormozd. The world bore witness to the fairness and national prosperity that prevailed during their reigns. Qobad was the heir to that empire. He was determined to uphold that tradition.

But these mobeds! Always busy hatching conspiracies. *Greedy creatures! Where has their purity gone? Good thoughts, good words, good deeds! Nothing good remains. If they have any goodness left, why don't they speak the truth? Why don't they acknowledge that the poor are dying from the famine? Dying of hunger?* "They were in this plight even before the famine struck the kingdom," the mobeds would likely say, stroking their long beards repeatedly. *Then why don't the landowners allocate a portion of their interest toward the welfare of the poor?* "Is it possible to levy a tax on grain?" they would answer. "Grain is transitory. It comes to an end. It rots away. But interest is permanent. Think about it—here, you impose tax, and there, grain runs out. So, what did we impose tax on? Something that isn't even there? Think about it, your majesty!" Qobad smiled sarcastically.

As he paced the room, he seemed to have forgotten the command he'd given earlier—that his most trusted guards and staff quietly and discreetly usher Seyavash into his private chamber that evening. He suddenly turned, and found Seyavash and Mazdak standing motionless at the doorway, framed by the curtains like figures in a portrait.

"Oh!" he exclaimed, his eyes immediately drawn to the newcomer's presence. The tall stranger was draped in a fine white cloak. He had ebony hair and a striking beard. His big, shiny black eyes, thick eyebrows, and delicate straight nose framed a mouth that exuded beneficence. Purity radiated from his countenance and demeanor, so much so that for a moment Qobad felt as if an angel had descended into his room. What kind of mobed was this? Unlike other priests, he had helped Qobad, and saved his life. Qobad was captivated by Mazdak at first sight.

The ordeals and searches Mazdak had endured while passing through the palace's labyrinths had left him astonished. This was the King's private chamber, where even his own son was forbidden from entering. The King was not supposed to meet anyone from the common public—only nobles.

"You do not even receive letters from your subjects. It is the ordinary officials who respond to them. No one is allowed to see you. This is the greatest plot devised against you by the priests and aristocrats—to isolate you from your oppressed, helpless, and loyal subjects." These were Mazdak's first words to Qobad after he had taken a seat.

"My subjects," Qobad repeated softly. "They are plagued with misfortunes at the moment. I want to help them, but . . . my statesmen . . . you do know they are conspiring to murder me."

"Illustrious king, statesmen are not the only ones who live in this kingdom. Win the support of the masses, and these high-ranking officials will not be able to harm you in the slightest."

"How?" asked Qobad.

"The statesmen wield power and influence because of their wealth. If you seize their riches and property, you will cripple them."

"They have their own infantry," said Qobad, deep in thought.

"Your general Shapur Mehran is loyal to you," replied Mazdak. "Open the doors to the nobles' warehouses. Your people are starving, suffering slow, agonizing deaths. Put the grain at their disposal and let each man take his share. Let the poor enter the palaces of the nobles."

Qobad listened to Mazdak with wide eyes. What harm could befall him if the nobles lost their wealth and power? Could he not join with his wretched subjects in laying the foundation for a just, prosperous, and mighty kingdom? Of course he could! His heart pounded at the thought.

"The farmers will seize my palace, too," he said.

"No," replied Mazdak, "they will shield it. They will not let any harm come to their great benefactor." Then, he smiled and added, "How much provision do you and your family need? How many sets of clothes?"

Qobad smiled back. "Not many. But," he said seriously, "I do need power, influence, authority. Without them . . ." he looked into the priest's dark, bright eyes.

"Without them, we will not accomplish a thing."

"It is now that you will know true power, your majesty. You will be like a magnificent, shady tree, and your subjects the trunk, roots, and foundation upon which the tree stands tall. A king's true infantry are his prosperous subjects. They will guard both kingdom and king."

Qobad looked at Seyavash, who met his gaze with affection, concern, and resolve.

"I am with you, mighty king. The commanders of your armies will stand by you. I have their ear and have been speaking to them in secret. Commander-in-chief Shapur Mehran does not wish to see the Persian empire dismantled. He does not want to witness yet another king's throne toppled. He is on your side."

He paused, then added dismissively: "We are not left with many options."

Any doubt or hesitation lingering in Qobad's heart and mind vanished.

"Well then?" he asked, raising his eyebrows, having come to a decision.

"Your Highness, according to the old almanac, Mah-e-Dozd is approaching," said Mazdak. "The Happy Day festival will be celebrated on the first of the month—a day when you are free to meet your people and speak with them. On that day, you will command the farmers to seize the granaries."

Seyavash's eyes danced with joy. "An excellent plan, mobed!" he exclaimed. The Happy Day festival was an ancient annual celebration in Persia. It was the day when the king descended from his throne and, clad in white, sat upon a white carpet. On this day, everyone in the kingdom was permitted to speak with him. The king conversed with farmers and landlords, and even partook in meals with them. During his conversation with his subjects, the king would declare: "Today, I am your equal, your brother. The subsistence and stability of this world depend on agriculture, and agriculture is entrusted to the government. Agriculture and government, then, are co-dependent. One cannot exist without the other."

Seyavash turned to Qobad: "I take it upon myself to ensure that on the appointed day, you are surrounded by a cavalry that is loyal to you. We will keep the aristocrats tied up elsewhere. They will not be allowed to come near you."

The commander and mobed stood. Qobad also rose, which was uncharacteristic of him. He seemed exceptionally happy. Seyavash and Qobad opened their arms and embraced warmly.

"This is an embrace between two friends," said Qobad, kissing Seyavash on the cheek. Then, he bowed before Mazdak. "Venerable, most worthy mobed! I am indebted to you."

He wanted to say that he would promote Mazdak to the highest rank of priesthood, but when he looked upon Mazdak's face, he hesitated. His countenance glowed with an ethereal calm. He was beyond such trivial concerns as riches and accolades. *What sort of being is this?* Qobad wondered with admiration. *It is my privilege to be in his company.*

As he walked away, Seyavash said: "Your Highness, the guards and staff who have seen us visiting with you tonight—along with your maidservant—must all be silenced before dawn."

"No!" said Mazdak, alarmed. "I refuse to be complicit in the murder of innocents for the sake of diplomacy."

"For heaven's sake, honored mobed!" Seyavash said with mild irritation. "Do not interfere in these matters. You have no knowledge of running the affairs of state. You are . . ."

"I refuse!" Mazdak persisted. "Ahura Mazda has declared the spilling of human blood to be the gravest of sins, especially that of an innocent."

"Right now, we must act on Ahura Mazda's other edict, not this one," Seyavash snapped.

Qobad laid a reassuring hand on Seyavash's shoulder and smiled, "I will have them put in solitary confinement." Then, he turned to Mazdak and added, "Temporarily, of course, supreme mobed."

"Oh!" Seyavash breathed a sigh of relief. He smiled, clasped Mazdak's arm, and left Qobad's room.

The final counsel needed was from the royal astrologer.

His head was crowned with a beautiful brocade turban, and he wore fine silken garments. Three strings of true pearls were wrapped around his neck, and his beard was immaculately trimmed. The closest confidant of kings and viziers, the astrologer sat upon a carpet with long reams of paper scattered around him. The papers were covered in intricate triangles and quadrilaterals, their margins filled with cryptic tables of numbers. The King sat in earnest, eager to hear what the astrologer had to reveal. Kings, princes, and officials alike never made any important decisions without first consulting him.

Royal astrologers had an ancient role in the Iranian empire. Their knowledge was based on the simple yet profound premise that the moon, sun, stars, planets, and the earth were all created from the same essence. That they were bound to each other and acted upon one another. The effect of the sun was evident to all, for without it, life on earth—flora and fauna alike—would be impossible. The influence of the moon's waxing and waning upon the sea was plainly visible, as observed by fisherfolk. But the other stars and planets were similarly in motion, alternately moving closer to and farther from the earth, from one another, and from the sun and moon. These celestial bodies influenced one another. To an astrologer's eye, all life on earth—from plants to beasts, birds, fish, and humans—was fashioned from the same essence as the sun, moon, and stars. Thus, all were bound to these celestial forces.

"But can this bond with the universe truly predict the future?" philosophers would ask them.

"If calculations are made correctly with analogical reasoning, then why not?" the astrologers answered. People might not have believed in them were it not for the fact that every prophecy they made about solar and lunar eclipses had come to pass. As a result, their loyal following included not only the nobility but also the common folk, and the astronomical charts they drew were highly regarded by both. Though commoners never had money to spare on astrologers, they had been reading the stars and making their own calculations for years. Standing in their little round canoes on the River Dujayl, the fishermen had been sharing their observations with the townsfolk for centuries: "When so-and-so star is positioned in such-and-such constellation, fish will flock this way!" They would lie on their backs upon the soft sands by the sea, eyes fixed upon the heavens, and steer their canoes east or west based on the stars' positions.

The royal astrologer bowed and kissed the carpet in obeisance to the King. Then, he said:

"Your Highness, my horoscope tables portend that you will live a long life. The Lord God will shelter you with His eternal mercy. It is not written in your destiny that you will surrender your life to your Maker in an unnatural manner. You will live a full, natural life, and, reposed on a comfortable bed in your palace, you will unite with your Maker."

"Hm!" said Qobad after a brief pause. Reassured, he stood up. His servants presented the royal astrologer with a golden tray brimming with jewels.

The King exited the royal hall. He was prepared for a new journey—one he had never undertaken before. *With farmers and laborers?* he thought. *Why not!* He answered his own question. He had ambition, and the force of life surged through his veins. *I'll show them.*

CHAPTER 10

"Come in, come in! Have a seat," Shapur welcomed Seyavash warmly, who stood respectfully beside a long, comfortable chair. The good-natured and gracious commander-in-chief of the King's cavalry, Shapur Mehran, had just returned the night before with a small caravan from Hirah. Tired from his travels, he had gone to bed early and had only just emerged from the bathhouse. Like the natives of Rum, he had on the long cotton cloak he typically wore around the house. He was quickly drying his hair with a soft cloth.

Upon receiving permission, Seyavash sat down deferentially on the edge of the chair. After many days of relentless effort, he had finally been granted leave to speak privately with the commander-in-chief.

"Hm! So, how are you, young man?" Shapur said as he settled into a plush velvet armchair. "What do you wish to tell me?" He then addressed his servant: "Go and have a delicious meal prepared." Turning to Seyavash, he laughed. "I've just come back from four days of drinking camel-milk, eating camel-meat, and staring at camels. I need to feel like I've returned to my world." He laughed heartily before continuing:

"No, no, I'm joking. The Arabs are very good, hospitable people, and loyal . . . I was there on an army inspection. I've returned having been introduced to a splendid language. Young man, have you ever heard Arabic? Granted, it's not as subtle or sweet as the Pahlavi tongue, but one can hear the whispers of the desert winds in it. Seyavash, have you ever considered that certain sounds from the environment find their way into languages? Sounds of the desert, of native birds, of gardens. I have heard that your mobed—what's his name? Mazdak? Yes, that Mazdak—offers thought-provoking reflections on the sounds of the tongue."

Seyavash leaned into the conversation eagerly. He felt comforted by the fact that the royal commander uttered Mazdak's name without a trace of contempt.

"You're absolutely right," he said respectfully.

"My son has told me about him," said Shapur, bursting into laughter: "Did you hear that? My son has become a Mazdakite! He claims that every single possession in the Sasanian kingdom should be shared equally among the people—even our palace! Hear me loud and clear, Seyavash: I am not giving away my property to anyone."

"My Lord, Sun King of the Empire, Star of the Persian sultanate, Mightiest of the Mighty, Monarch of Monarchs," began Seyavash.

"Enough!" said Shapur, irritated. "Are you keeping company with the scribes, by any chance? Since they're paid by the page, they've discovered a way to fill endless pages with honorifics. They cram tens and tens of pages with titles and flourishes, and make the subject matter so lengthy and complicated that an ordinary soldier cannot hope to understand the simplest of orders."

Mustering his courage, Seyavash replied: "Venerable Lord, nobles and priests are vanishing from the capital."

"Hm!" the commander-in-chief exhaled slowly. "Excellent. Let us send them a message—they would do well not to return."

Shapur Mehran stood up restlessly and began to pace the room with slow, deliberate steps. "Did they truly think they could face the King's cavalry with the ordinary troops they raised on their own lands? I was not present when the cursed, hell-bound Zarmeher proposed a plan for . . . may it never come to pass . . . regicide, or I would not have left his head upon his shoulders for a single moment longer. It took time, but at least this good deed is now done. It is lamentable that these officials, in their folly, have busied themselves with plotting yet another disturbance in the realm. Do we not have enough to contend with? Our adversaries are keeping tabs on us. Our enemy, Hunan, lies in wait, seizing our lands. Rum has stationed its troops at the border. Our people languish in misery . . ." Shapur trailed off, absorbed in thought. After a pause, he spoke slowly and deliberately:

"Young man . . . my forefathers won the Persian empire by spilling their lifeblood, through exceptional physical prowess. One of my ancestors conquered Bakhtarayah and Sistan, and the magnificent river that flows through these lush, verdant mountains and pastures bears his name—Mehran. Since the dawn of time, we have been regents and stewards to kings. How could we stand idle and watch this kingdom undone? And this mobed, Mazdak . . . he calls himself a prophet of God. His religion . . ."

"Great king, his religion is the same as ours," Seyavash interjected. "He says that he is striving for its perfection."

"Anyhow," Shapur Mehran lifted a hand, silencing Seyavash. "He is popular among the subjects. Join forces with the people and strengthen the kingdom. What harm could come of that? If his religion helps fortify the realm, we will offer him protection. Religions that stabilize and expand the kingdom are important." His thoughts drifted. "I believe that religion and state are one. Religion reflects the grandeur of the state . . . no, what am I saying? I mean to say that the state itself is a testament to the splendor and glory of religion." Suddenly, he asked: "Is Mazdak a Manichaean?"

"No, Your Highness," Seyavash replied hesitantly. "To my knowledge, Mazdak is not a Manichaean."

"Anyway, what difference does it make?" said Shapur, spreading his arms. "Shapur I—my namesake and one of the great Persian kings—gave Mani his full protection. Under his reign, Manichaeism flourished and spread far and wide. The Arab king of Hirah, Amr ibn Adi also advocated for the Manichaean cause, which strengthened the state and bolstered Hirah's alliance with Fars. So, dear boy, religion is for the State. Now look at Constantinople, reinforcing the state with Christianity. Otherwise . . ." he lowered his voice, "that poor soul—they had him . . . what do they say . . . crucified. And don't forget, my friend, when was Christianity revealed to Constantine? On the battlefield, among cross-shaped clouds, he heard a voice: *if you want to win the battle, become Christian*. And so, he became Christian. Religion helped the cavalry, didn't it?"

The young commander listened to his senior with rapt attention, as a pupil listens to a master. He asked:

"Pray tell, is the present sovereign of Hirah a Manichaean?"

"Who? Munzir? Their Shah? No, he is not Manichaean."

Shapur then launched into a tale relating his discoveries during the recent visit to Hirah. "Son, did you know that the inhabitants of Hirah to the south are not idol-worshippers? They belong to a sect called the Hanifs. They are monotheists, like us, and believe in one God—though they call Him by a different name. A word that lingers in my memory but escapes my tongue at the moment.

Very similar to the Hebrew word 'Elohim.' Like us, they believe God is heavenly light.

"Which reminds me," he continued, "a caravan of Sabaeans visited Hirah while I was there. They trade in a fragrant wood of the finest quality. I bought an entire bundle from them. I will give you some to present to Mazdak. If he puts it in the sacred fire, his entire fire-temple will be perfumed."

"Indeed, very good!" Seyavash said, bowing his head.

"As I was saying, the Sabaeans believe that light and darkness are forever locked in an eternal struggle, as do we. Lohrasp told me—he lived there for many years and knows the desert tongues. It is a marvel to hear his Arya tongue turn so easily on the sounds of their language. Ha!" He laughed. "Lohrasp would often converse with the trading caravans. He told me that the Sabaeans' faith in the struggle between good and evil is much like ours. In fact, I assumed they belonged to a sect of our own religion—except they do not revere and worship fire. Lohrasp says that in their kingdom—yes, they have a small realm of their own, perhaps the size of one of our small provinces—there is a structure they consider sacred, like our fire-temple. It is square-shaped and possibly houses a black stone. Of course, this is all based on hearsay; I have not seen it with my own eyes. But I do know that, like us, they also possess a holy scripture."

Seyavash wanted to leave, but it would have been disrespectful to depart before the commander-in-chief had finished sharing his thoughts. He felt confident that the general and his army would help, not harm, his two dear friends Qobad and Mazdak. Shapur was about to signal that Seyavash could go, when suddenly he remembered something.

"The Shah of the Sabaeans was their chief mobed, whom they call *mukarrib*. But what do mobeds know of kingship? Mobeds are making our lives miserable, son. I can't even appoint a knight in my cavalry without their permission. Affairs of the state are beyond their comprehension, yet they refuse to stay out of them. They spend all their time collecting debts and calculating interest, when in fact, my boy . . ." he stroked his beard slowly, continuing, "if one considers the established practices of our faith carefully, mobeds are not permitted to engage in business or trade. Everything they are doing is contrary to the faith."

"Indeed!" Seyavash nodded. It struck him as curious that the practice of dispensing loans and charging interest had its origins in the fire-temples themselves. The priests had amassed such wealth from the lavish gifts given them by nobles and the meager offerings of the poor that they began lending grain to trading caravans journeying to other cities and kingdoms for business. They retained a portion of the profit for themselves. Soon, they extended loans of both coins and grain to ordinary shopkeepers and laborers. While this offered no advantage to the debtors, collecting interest from them became a priority. When, for instance, a debtor's house burned down and he sought a loan to rebuild it, he was told he must pay the principal along with interest.

"But why?" the debtor would ask.

"Because you will earn a profit," the mobeds replied.

"How is that?"

"You build a house, sleep fitfully, go to work in the morning, earn a living. Tell me, then, do you not earn a profit?"

The poor debtor—whether he was a builder, or farmer, or miner—was left speechless by this clever logic. He would take the loan, bound in servitude to the mobed for life.

Similarly, synagogues in Rum were issuing loans on a grand scale. Mobeds and pastors continuously lent money to the poor. The cycle was the same for everyone: spiritual leaders loaned money to the needy, while also issuing debts to high-ranking officials and aristocrats, whose coffers were often drained by extravagant spending.

Shapur Mehran said: "It's necessary to curtail the power of the mobeds. When peace with the enemy is crucial, they force us to wage war; and when the time comes for battle, they persuade their loyal, subservient commanders to enter into absurd pacts with the enemy. I am willing to drink sulphur, even to walk on hot coals, to prove that I speak the truth: the pact Zarmeher made with Hunan was a grave mistake. It was insidious, disgraceful. The mobeds took a bribe from Hunan. And now, with Rum eager to sink its teeth into a magnificent city like Nusaybin, the mobeds insist on waging war with Hunan. The question is, who is the true and greater enemy: the relatively harmless Hunan, or the formidable Rum empire? It is the latter that poses a genuine threat. As for the Huns, I could make them a division of my army in a heartbeat," he boasted.

Seyavash thought that the Huns—whose barbaric attacks had shaken the whole Sasanian empire—was hardly as harmless as Shapur seemed to believe. Yet it was true that forming an alliance with them against Rum would be far easier. It was a sensible plan. Perhaps Yazd was at work. Meanwhile, Shapur Mehran remained absorbed in thoughts of the mobeds' unseemly behavior. Suddenly, he brightened up and said:

"I met the chief mobed and his Jewish accountants at a gathering. The chief mobed was giving a discerning speech on the forces of the universe. Can you imagine what he said? He claimed that, no doubt, myriad forces are at work in the cosmos, but the greatest force of all, as you know, is compound interest!" Shapur burst out laughing, then suddenly grew somber and forlorn. "The root cause of poverty . . ." he murmured, before adding, "You may leave now."

Bearing gifts wrapped in precious bags, Seyavash departed from Shapur Mehran's opulent palace.

CHAPTER 11

King Qobad with the starving farmers during the Happy Day festival.

Seyavash stood a few feet from Qobad's white carpet, flanked by his vigilant cavalry. On the floor among the crowd sat Mazdak, draped in a cloak of pure white. His head was tucked between his knees, and he appeared to be lost in deep meditation.

"O Lord Almighty, Ahura Mazda, Wise and Supreme God, Maker of the Universe! Grant me the courage and perseverance to speak what my heart and mind perceive with clarity. Are these thoughts not from You? Truly, it is Your divine light, a message entrusted to my safekeeping."

His eyes remained closed, his hands clenched into fists. He drew three deep breaths. Then, he rose to his feet, his face the very picture of calm. He lifted his right hand. A hush swept over the crowd, every ear attuned to his words.

"I, Mazdak, am a prophet of God. I bring a message from Him. Listen carefully."

A strangled cry of amazement rose from the crowd.

"The exalted prophet Zoroaster came to me in a waking dream. He said that the God of the two worlds, in His boundless mercy and beneficence, has filled the earth with the means of life, so that all creation may share them equally, and none may take more than another."

The crowd stood in stunned silence.

"But disparity was forced upon humanity by Ahriman. Misled by his wickedness, each of you sought to seize one another's share to satisfy your own desires. This inequality is the source of all misery in the world; in its name, people fight, lie, plunder, and shed one another's blood. Zoroaster said that for thousands of years, humanity has roamed the earth in a wretched state because of this very disparity."

A thousand eyes were fixed on Mazdak's face, a thousand ears straining to catch his every word.

"Inequality breeds inequality. Covetousness does not bring contentment; it spawns an endless cycle of greed. That is Ahriman's doing, not God's. God is benevolence, peace, and beauty. He is light. He has granted no one the right to take more than another, as Zoroaster said."

The crowd stood in hypnotic silence. Mazdak's voice rose, louder and more resolute than before.

"Hence, it is necessary that wealth be taken from the rich and given to the poor. We must restore the equality that reigned among humanity at the dawn of Creation."

All Mazdak could hear was the distant murmur of a faraway commotion, and all his eyes could see was a wavering mist.

"My friends, hear this message. Write it down, commit it to memory, lest the world claim tomorrow that a prophet—failed to deliver God's true and final word to His people—Arya and Hebrew alike," warned Mazdak.

Then his vision cleared, and the world returned to focus. In a serene voice, he said:

"Like water, fire, and pastures, so too must wealth be held in common. It is a virtue ordained by God, and He shall reward it in abundance. When we free one another from encumbrances, the Lord will elevate us and favor our mutual accord."

The mob stood speechless. Not far off, a horde of hungry, half-clad farmers, laborers, skilled workers, and townsmen listened to Mazdak's words with astonishment and disbelief, as the King's guard repeated them aloud for all to hear.

Now Mazdak turned toward King Qobad and said, "My King, do you consent? Will you yourself obey, and lead your subjects in obedience to God's command?"

Qobad rose and said:

"O Prophet of God , I bow my head in submission before His command."

Then Qobad turned to address the people:

"I am your brother. While your stomachs are empty, the very thought of having food or water is like poison to me. I, Qobad, King of Persia, invested with full power and authority over this realm, grant you permission to take food for yourself and your innocent children from the nobles' granaries."

These were Qobad's words, not God's—words of worldly power, of majesty, of dominion—yet they had turned the hope and tears borne of the divine Word into unwavering faith. The mood of the gathering changed. Pallor gave way to radiant joy. Arms were waving in the air, bodies leapt with sudden optimism, and a roar rose from the crowd:

"Long live Qobad, King of Kings!"

The first horde of starving peasants advanced toward the nobles' havelis, Seyavash and his troops marching at their side. The guards at the gates couldn't stop them; lowering their maces and swords, they stepped aside. The padlocks of the first haveli were broken, then the second, and the third. *Dhal, dhal, dhal,* went the grain as it poured into tattered sacks—barley, wheat, fine rice from distant provinces, corn, lentils.

Farmers hurried to their huts to fetch pots, bringing their wives and children along. They lit their stoves from the sacred fire and bowed in reverence before it.

O holy fire—
image of the divine, purifier of all matter,
lightning in the clouds, heat of the sun,
warmth of the body, sign of life—
warmth, that mingles with the hallowed moisture of
 the jungles,
giving new life to the deadened, black soil,
from which bursts a virgin bud—pure, unsullied—
 that was never before.
O sacred fire! You are without limit,
the very image of Ahura Mazda!
Glory! Glory! All glory to Ahura Mazda!

Hymns of praise ascended from the farmers' huts.

CHAPTER 12

Across the vast, lush plains that stretched to the fine line of the horizon, Commander Goshtasp rode like the wind. His pedigreed stallion galloped with all its might, foam flecking its mouth, its hoofs barely touching the earth. Goshtasp snapped the reins, leaning so low that his face brushed the horse's mane as it whipped in the wind. Horse and rider raced forward, cleaving the air while dusty gusts buffeted their faces. It seemed as though both had fused into one being, hurtling ahead with such speed and unity that they became the very image of a single, unstoppable force in motion.

About three miles behind, in fierce pursuit, rode Barzin. His untamed hair streamed in the wind, his heels pressed hard into the horse's flanks, and with teeth clenched, he spurred the horse onward. The ground seemed to tremble beneath the pounding of their hoofs.

"Barzin!" Goshtasp shouted. "I am Azar Goshtasp! Do you know the meaning of my name? Fire of the Sasanian warrior kings, symbol of the kingdom's might and splendor!" The wind carried his voice straight to Barzin. Like the clouds of dust, it filled his mouth, his ears, and his nose.

"And my name is Azar Barzin," Barzin shouted with all his strength. "Do you know what that means? Fire of the farmers—

and I will not spare you!" His voice scattered in the dust-filled air, flung far into the distance. Goshtasp wheeled around and drew the bowstring back to his ear. The poisoned arrow hissed through the air and buried itself in the forehead of Barzin's horse. The next arrow penetrated its neck. The horse neighed loudly, reared on its hind legs, then crashed to the ground. Barzin struggled beneath its crushing weight before wrenching himself free. Blood pooled beneath the fallen horse's muzzle, soaking the earth.

"No! No!" Barzin screamed as he watched Goshtasp riding off, quickly becoming a dot on the horizon. The horse bucked twice or thrice, then became still. Barzin threw himself against the horse and sobbed hysterically. He looked around. The plains were deserted. Not a soul could be seen. Barzin stood up. *There is nobody here. What will I do now?*, he wondered, worried. He started running as fast as he could, got tangled in a bush, and fell. Barzin sat up. *I wish an animal would appear that I could ride back on . . . a cow or something . . .* His eyes searched far and wide, hoping to catch sight of a ride.

Barzin's paternal grandfather had once told him that in ancient times, a handful of people mounted a strange-looking cow called Sarasvag and set out on a journey. They traversed the heavenly territories, which no man could hope to reach by any other means. One night, just as they were crossing the middle of the sea, the wind tossed the three fires burning on the cow's back into the waves. But like three life forms, the fires reignited on the cow's back, precisely where they had been burning before. Fighting the disappointment that had overcome him, Barzin shouted: "Mother! O holy mother!"

"Arre arre! What's wrong? What is happening?" Barzin's wife shook him awake. He opened his eyes. His throat was parched.

What was all this? Where was he? For a few moments, he was very confused. Then, slowly and steadily, his vision cleared. The thin mat he was lying on and the walls of his mud house came into focus. His three children lay sleeping on another mat.

It was a dream, Barzin realized. He asked his wife for some water, took a few sips, and sat up in bed. "I had a dream," he told his wife.

"What was the dream? You were scared. Tell me about it."

"Tell you? No, you're not an interpreter. Dreams . . . they shouldn't be related to just anyone. I need to see Prophet Mazdak. Tomorrow."

"Am I 'just anyone'? Me?"

"No . . . you're not 'just anyone,'" Barzin wrapped his arms around his youthful wife and fell onto the bed. "You are my Quz Banu. My king-wife! Ha!" he laughed. "Can poor folk like us have a king-wife? Sure! Why not?"

Then, he said: "I had a dream . . . that I'm running like the wind . . . no, that I'm on horseback, and the horse is running like the wind . . . and I draw the bowstring, but the arrow flies backward, carried in the opposite direction by a gust of wind, when in fact . . ." he laughed out loud, then continued, "neither do I know horseback riding, nor archery . . . but it felt exactly like I was riding the horse. I was pulling at the reins. My mind remembers it so vividly. The tension in the bowstring, the arrow leaving the bow!" Barzin recalled in a daze.

His wife stroked his face with love and concern, "Don't worry." She pulled the tattered sheet over Barzin, then huddled in beside him. The light from their fireplace danced on the walls of the mud house. She ran her fingers through Barzin's thick, curly hair, and said: "Dreams always have the opposite meaning."

"Who told you that?" Barzin asked anxiously.

"My mother's father," she replied.

"Ah, your grandfather!" said Barzin. He felt reassured. In his mind, he believed that the words spoken by their elders were true. The ones who came before their elders, or those who had passed on possessed even greater wisdom. At a subconscious level, he was aware that knowledge and wisdom did not completely pass on from one generation to another. Humans were capable of bequeathing only a fraction of their wisdom and knowledge to their children. The rest was dispersed, left behind. Many important teachings are forgotten with the dead. Just like the overflowing bags of grain that the miners were hauling back and forth these days—the excess grain spilled over, getting quashed under sand and dust. Only the people who were extremely needy would retrace their steps and go back to sift through the dirt for the spilled provisions. Most miners forgot all about the fallen grain. They would hurriedly grind whatever grain had made it to their homes so they could make *chapatis*—flatbread—or go out again the next day in search of fresh grain. Barzin imagined that for centuries, mankind had been carrying sacksful of knowledge and worldly wisdom upon its back. A great deal of it must have spilled out of the bags over the course of the journey.

Barzin gently caressed his wife's body. In the past, she had served three high-ranking officials; the father of one of their children—their daughter—was a *marzban*, a commander of the border guards. Barzin nuzzled his face in the crook of his wife's neck. His gaze fell upon his tools hanging on a wall—a hammer and chisel. The flames smoldering in an earthen pot inside their fire temple cast a glow on the tools, the shadows of light rising and falling on the wall. The hammer and chisel seemed to move in the rippling firelight. The glimmering implements reminded Barzin of Derafsh Kaviani—the Kaviani banner—symbol of the Sasanid kings. *Wasn't it the flag of a blacksmith, a forger, who defeated the demon-king Zahhak? Zahhak, the evil tyrant, who used to smear human brains on his boils daily. The blacksmith's army captured him and rid the Aryan empire of his tyranny. But then . . .* Barzin meditated *. . . then the blacksmith tracked down the Ashkanian prince Feraydun, and put him on the throne. Why? Why didn't Kaveh crown himself? How would things have turned out if a blacksmith had ascended to the throne? Then the forger would have become king. Is that what I want? No, never! We'll have to find another way . . .*

Barzin sensed an unknown power flowing in his arms. He began to caress his wife, breathing heavily and whispering urgently in her ear, "You are mine. Mine!" He repeated this over and over until his wife replied in surprise: "Arre, yes, yes. Did I not say that I'm yours?" Barzin halted. He became lost in thought. Then, he nestled his face in his wife's neck and began to laugh quietly. Indeed! What did he think his wife was? Harmony on earth?

The miner and his wife went back to sleep for the remainder of the night.

CHAPTER 13

Every follower of Zoroastrianism knew that the Day of Reckoning was coming. When the world would end, and the dead would be resurrected. The Zoroastrian faith described the arrival of Judgement Day like this: the comet "Gočihr" would fall on earth, causing an explosion that would light the earth on fire; all metals would melt in the intense heat of the fire, and this fiery flood of molten lava would engulf the world. This would be Doomsday.

But Doomsday was already upon them. In Rozmeher's palace, and in the countless other palaces of Ctesiphon. Rozmeher's family, his two beautiful, delicate young daughters, his aging king-wife, several subordinate wives, dozens of domestic servants and attendants all stood in a queue on the secret spiral staircase made of red sandstone. They were quivering with fear. The stairway led all the way up to Rozmeher's bed chamber. Downstairs, the mob of filthy, wretched farmers, masons, and miners was feverishly looting Rozmeher's resplendent guest rooms. There was a loud racket as they turned the priceless rarities strewn around the house upside down, utterly unaware of their value. Articles were tossed into the air as the peasants flung them frantically into the giant sacks their wives had sewn together in a hurry.

A carpenter glanced at the stairway. He leaped forward and grabbed Rozmeher's daughter by her wrist.

"I'll have this one," he said in a hoarse voice. "She'll be my wife."

Rozmeher's whole body shook with anger. "Let go of her! You savages! You break into my home, and now you violate my honor!"

Leaning his back against a pillar stood Barzin. He said: "Rozmeher, your daughters from your subordinate wives are living in peasants' homes today, because according to your custom, only sons from your subordinate wives are allowed to enter your homes. One of your daughters, whose biological father is a commander of the border guards, is being raised in my home as my daughter. Why all this commotion?"

"Silence!" Rozmeher thundered. "That is a tradition among noble families. If you had the capacity to understand, you'd realize that you've committed a grave sin by barging into my private home. You hell-bound wretch!"

All this time, the miner was in distress. He did not like what he saw. But Rozmeher's words and the thought of his ties to Zarmeher infuriated him. "Rozmeher, for centuries your despicable servants have broken into our homes the same way. They would tear down the reed mats from our doors with the tips of their bayonets and barge inside. They pilfered our broken pots and pans, and threw our worn sheets and mattresses into disarray. They even dug up our floors to inspect if we had stolen something from them and buried it in the earth. They dragged away our wives and sisters in front of our eyes to offer them to you. Were those not our private homes and shacks? Were we . . . not human? But of course! I'm a miner, he's a dirty laborer—we cannot think. We don't have the capacity to think."

"You . . . you!" sputtered Rozmeher. "You have been accustomed to this for centuries . . . you can't have minded it! Why do you compel me to open my mouth . . . you couldn't have been happier about your women entering our harems. You would use them to ask us for small favors in exchange—relief from interest, permission for loan repayment extensions . . ."

The half-truth in Rozmeher's words struck Barzin's face like a slap. But it wasn't the complete truth. They were treated disgracefully and humiliated, and if someone had learned to find happiness in disgrace and humiliation, he was no more than a worm that enjoys wallowing in the dirt. These high-ranking officers and nobles had turned them into worms, birthed by Ahriman.

"Now your daughters will ask us to do you small favors," hissed Barzin. Then, he turned to the carpenter: "Take the girl. She's yours."

"I won't keep her to myself," said the carpenter triumphantly. "We will all share her. She'll be our joint property. What do you say, my friends?"

In the ancient Sasanid kingdom, sharing wives, loaning them to friends, offering them to the nobles to be taken as subordinate wives—willingly or forcefully—was nothing unusual for this mob. They paid no heed to what the carpenter had just said, as they sat on the floor, guzzling Rozmeher's expensive wine.

But Rozmeher heard every single word. He pondered in astonished rage. *Women? Now they were going to make women their joint property. Nobody would know who the father of a child was. Alas! Would ancestral identity disappear from the Aryan empire?*

In Rozmeher's eyes, that was the most odious perversion of God's decree. Everyone knew that ancestry had blurred over the ages, yet in the gilded margins of such a society they were safe, too. Each participant was aware and accepting of the tradition that the son of a high-ranking officer would be a high-ranking officer, the son of a mobed would be a mobed, and the son of a noble would be a noble. That the son would propagate the father's heritage. *These scoundrels are bent upon mixing nobility with filth. Our kingdom will become a hellhole. My paternal cousin Zarmeher wasn't wrong in proposing that we kill this half-mad king who has aligned himself with Mazdak! Ah! If only his plan had succeeded . . . but Shapur Mehran . . . that cursed Shapur Mehran had Zarmeher killed. We will not spare his life. We are here, we are alive!*

"Up, get up!" Barzin said dejectedly. "Let's go . . . enough drinking . . . it's a different time, completely different . . . flinging things here and there . . . this is not a gathering for wine-drinking."

He headed toward the door and was about to leave when he paused. He turned, and said in a low voice: "Let the girl go."

The carpenter scowled. Barzin left.

But that month, many girls were snatched from the havelis and palaces.

CHAPTER 14

That day, blood spilled for the first time on the sweeping path to Ctesiphon.

The path emerged from Ctesiphon and led to the city of Istakhr in the province of Fars. Before now, this path had been used only by the extravagantly decorated chariots, drawn by two or four horses, belonging to the splendid havelis and estates that lined the road. High-spirited armed cavalrymen guarded these lands astride their horses, and the air reverberated with the intimidating chorus of horses' hoofs. But today, this path was crowded with builders, miners, and farmers brandishing spears, lances, spades, axes, hammers. They were tearing down the granaries of a haveli and looting its treasures as the landowner attempted to flee with his family and private army. There was pandemonium on the highway, and nobody could hear a sound over the din. Women, toward the back of the throngs, pushed the men forward with all their might.

With a grinding sound, the wheel of a chariot spun off. The chariot tilted to one side and toppled. The passengers screamed, trying desperately to cling to their seats. A few laborers sought to drag the delicate handmaidens off the chariot, but the gleaming swords of the armed troops stalled their hands. Several people in the crowd suffered deep wounds on their arms, chests, and faces. The crowd tried to reattach the wheel to the chariot's wooden peg. Finally, it slid back on and the chariot resumed its motion.

Barzin stood watching from a sloping flight of stone steps, surprised and distressed at the scene before him. In the commotion he was unable to recognize a single face. Droplets of perspiration trickled from his forehead into his eyes, which he kept wiping off with the lower front of his worn-out shirt. Mustering up all his strength, he tried to yell:

"Stop, stop!"

But his throat was dry. The highway was in an uproar, and even the people rushing by right in front of him could not hear his weak voice.

Some scribes had also ended up in the crowd. Driven to desperation by their starving families, they were compelled into joining the plunderers. They carried big pots to fill with grain. The mob of sturdy builders was pushing them back repeatedly. An out-of-breath scribe sank down at Barzin's feet. He was holding on to his pot resolutely.

"Stop!" Barzin tried to shout again. The scribe looked up at him. Then, he panted, "Your shirt. Wave your shirt."

Barzin instantly took his shirt off and waved it vigorously in the air. A builder or two caught sight of him. A miner recognized Barzin and ran over to him.

"Where is it? Where is your pot?"

Barzin raced down the stairs and grabbed his arm.

"Meher Shah! Meher Shah! You can't do this."

"I can't do this?" Meher Shah bristled. "The honorable Messenger has granted us his permission. Don't you see? Our people have been butchered here."

He paused, then continued: "These landlords and their families. We wouldn't have taken their lives. Two days ago, a family of nobles left here with their private army, killing farmers and craftsmen along the way to Istakhr. They massacred three miners and a blacksmith. After covering some distance, their own army turned on them and murdered everyone, down to the last child, and made off with the carts filled with their belongings—gold, silver, weapons. The slain bodies of the nobles are still lying on the main road to Istakhr. Jackals and hyenas are making a feast of them."

"Even slaughtered the women!" Barzin was scandalized. Faith decreed that taking a weapon to a woman was an unforgivable sin.

"The women?" Meher Shah laughed in a deadpan manner. "No, they took the women with them. To share with each other."

"Meher Shah," Barzin pleaded, "we must go to the Great Messenger. Today, this very moment. Tonight. Let's gather about a hundred miners. We need to spread the message from house to house. No, not just the miners," he added, his thoughts racing. "Assemble some farmers, too. Craftsmen as well." Suddenly, he was struck with an idea. He leaped at the scribe sitting on the stone step below.

"We don't know how to write," said Barzin. "What's your name?"

"Narsi. I've got nothing. Look!" The scribe showed Barzin his empty pot.

"I'll get it filled right away," Barzin announced. "You'll accompany us tonight."

Hauling the pot, Meher Shah darted toward the haveli's granaries.

The scribe's gaze swept over the crowd, apprehensive. But when Meher Shah returned, pushing his way through and dragging the scribe's pot, now filled to the brim with barley and millet, a wave of relief and joy washed over his face. He got to his feet and kneeled before Meher Shah, thanking and praising him.

"The acolytes of Meher Shah are forever grateful. May the earth and sky sing your praises each moment, O Supreme Slave of God!"

"You'll come along with us," Barzin interrupted severely.

"O Lord of Fruit, Trees, and Stars!" the scribe spoke humbly. "I have to get home! My wife is feeling—"

"Do you see this?" Meher Shah waved the ax in front of the scribe's face. "It can shatter stone. Your bony neck would be no match. I'm a miner."

In the distance, the thunder of horses' hooves and the cracking of whips heralded the riders of the Sasanid army.

The crowd in front of the haveli scattered.

Lifting his eyes to the sky, the scribe conceded. "I'll come." He tried to lift the heavy pot of grain.

"I shall carry it," said Meher Shah. "That way I can see your house, too." They departed.

Barzin watched them till they disappeared. Then, startled, he turned his attention to the approaching troops.

The silver border on the archer's shalwar gleamed, his head adorned with a plumed turban. His officers recognized Barzin because of his close ties to the Messenger. They trusted him. With a nod, the archer summoned Barzin.

"What happened over here?"

"This family was headed to Istakhr," explained Barzin.

"Hmm," the archer said. "Did they kill anyone?"

"No. Some people were wounded."

The archer urged his horse forward. As he was riding off, he called, "Why are they going to Fars? Their farmers have rebelled as well, even though there is no famine over there. There is news of rain from all over Fars. Miners! Even the tribes of the late Shah Balash from Sistan have joined our cause!"

Barzin listened closely to the archer, then began his journey home. He had heard this as well, even though he didn't have any time for rumors during those tumultuous days. Word was going around that Mazdak's message was spreading in the province of Fars, as well as by the coast, in Makran and Sistan. Farmers and the working class were beginning to support him. What's more, the Kings' tribes had joined Mazdak's following, jubilant that the chief mobeds and nobles of the fire temples, who had overpowered several kings, were being stripped of their powers as kingmakers. In Ctesiphon, too, hundreds of fire temples had been closed. Only three great temples remained, of which one was frequented by the Messenger himself.

"An abundance of houses of worship defiles faith," he would say.

Barzin smiled contentedly.

Suddenly, his train of thought broke. His house stood before him, and his children were playing out front. They ran over to Barzin.

"What did you bring? What did you bring for us?!"

"Nothing. I can't bring something every day. You ate, didn't you?" Barzin stroked the children's dark ringlets, took his little daughter in his arms, and entered the house.

Inside, his wife was grinding flour. A lock of ebony hair swayed over her fair cheeks.

"Mehrin," said Barzin. His wife was still so beautiful—a firm body, radiant black eyes, rosy lips. When she cooked, her face flushed pink from the heat of the fire.

Mehrin raised her eyes and looked at him, then looked around him. "I'll get lunch ready," she said, assured that Barzin had not brought anything for her to put away.

Barzin set down his daughter and sat on a charpoy. The mattress had been folded away. A glass of water on the mantel held a single rose.

Barzin laughed. "I didn't bring anything."

"Good," Mehrin replied. "We still have grain left in the house." Then, she raised an eyebrow and said with feigned coquetry: "I am afraid that one day you might bring home a Harbaz beauty with you."

Barzin laughed heartily. "I know you would poison her!"

Mehrin gathered the flour, heaped some in a tray, and poured water on it. She laughed gaily as she kneaded the dough. "Not quite."

Mehrin had been a guest in the houses of nobility. Even in those days, she would secretly meet Barzin. Two teardrops formed within the depths of Barzin's heart, but he restrained them. "Oh, darling! I have never even laid eyes on anyone else."

Mehrin was firing up the tandoor. They would have to wait a while for the oven to get hot.

Barzin took off his shoes. Everything he had said was a lie, but a man has to lie to his wife. In the beginning, there had been other women, noblewomen who had been taken political prisoners. He had never taken them in his home . . . but in a grove of trees in the woods . . . in a deserted haveli behind pillars. Each time, he returned with a sense of loss. What were those beautiful women to him but puppets of flesh? Even his virility was diminishing with time, which terrified him. He wasn't acquainted with such fragile maidens, who wept while he was with them. "I will give you to a kind-natured builder or farmer," he assured them. He missed Mehrin.

Mehrin! His mother had never met her. Mehrin was not a Kurd like him. Her ancestors had migrated from Fars to Ctesiphon. They were builders, and so many magnificent monuments were under construction at all times in the capital city of the Sasanian kingdom that there was a job for every builder in the sultanate. This is where Barzin had seen her for the first time, drawing water at a well. When they found out that Barzin had no family, Mehrin's mother and father gladly arranged their daughter's wedding with him.

He was happy with his only wife—very happy. Barzin had built this mud house with his own hands using straw and dirt, and Mehrin's presence filled it with a soft glow.

She placed a vegetable mash and naan before him.

"You should eat as well," said Barzin, placing the first bite in her mouth.

"Hunh!" Mehrin laughed, her mouth full of food. "Then who will make the naan?" She turned toward the tandoor.

Barzin ate hastily. "I better go," he said.

There's an important task. I have to alert the people. Tonight. We'll meet our noble Messenger. I need to inform them first.

Finishing his meal, Barzin filled a vessel with water and strode out of his mud house.

He rinsed his mouth, face, and hands. Then he washed his feet. "O feet!" he exclaimed. "You have a lot of work to do today." He dipped his fingers in the water and ran them over his arms up to his elbows, then performed *masah*. This was a holy ritual to be completed before the worship of fire. He was about to embark upon a sacred mission. He was certain of it.

CHAPTER 15

That night, the Messenger's haveli was full of builders, miners, and craftsmen. They were sitting on the ground, by the pillars, on the shriveled grass, and on the parapet surrounding the pond. They were far more than one hundred in number. As soon as anybody heard that Hazrat Mazdak was issuing orders on how to bring this great revolution about the right way, they instantly joined his band of followers. Thousands of builders, craftsmen, and farmers were now weary of looting and plundering. This wasn't their ancestral vocation, it was the livelihood of bandits who lived in hiding up in the pitch-black mountains of Bisutun and raided the caravans traveling on the sprawling highways of the kingdom. But they were under great duress from hunger. They were also vexed by the realization that some of them had begun to take pleasure in the pillaging. Another important detail was that only those with physical prowess got a share in the grain and property. Was there another way? They all wanted to know.

In a sculptured verandah of the haveli, carpets were pulled out from the drawing room and laid underneath an archway. Mazdak sat cross-legged on a carpet in the center. On his left sat the scribe with several inkpots and reams of paper, and people were surprised to see Mazdak's Jewish friend Joshwa sitting on his right.

Mazdak and Joshwa were deep in conversation, speaking in whispers with heads huddled.

"It was for this very day that he became an accountant," someone in the crowd murmured. "How did his father allow him to come?"

"He settles the mobeds' accounts, and skins us alive collecting compound interest," whispered another.

"Look, many sons of influential fathers are sitting here," Barzin said happily in a low voice.

Among the crowd was Prince Kavus, clinging to the plinth of a column. Despite the builders' and craftsmen's insistence, he had refused to sit on a carpet. He must have been barely seventeen years old. He was an ardent advocate of Mazdak, enraptured by the idea of equality. Equality, which he had never experienced in the seventeen years of his life. Equality, which evoked a pleasure rarer than alcohol . . . "As if this purposeless life has been endowed with meaning!" he would repeat to himself quietly. "It's like I've been released from captivity!" Captive in the palace, captive in the royal carriage, captive while walking in the gardens. Ushers, sentinels, handmaids every moment, every instant, whose bodies were so alike that he couldn't recognize their faces. "Didn't you come to me last night? Oh, was that someone else?" he'd say listlessly. Granted, some bodies were fair, and some dark. But which body belonged to which face? As soon as he turned fifteen, Kavus suspected that he was becoming afflicted with amnesia, like a ninety-year-old infirm. But that was not the case. He was just dejected. His youthful mind was at the threshold of childhood and maturity. All five senses were animated. He could recognize the faces and voices of his companions from a distance. He knew their names, the ways to their houses, what they did for a living.

Suddenly, Mazdak's voice boomed. It was the clear, resounding, cultured voice of an eminent mobed. The buzz in the crowd died instantly.

"Farmers, craftsmen, miners! You must stop looting immediately! Plundering will only ensure that the powerful end up with all the property and grain. King Qobad's army is collecting grain in the official godowns. It will be delivered to your houses each month as needed. Spend it economically."

The Messenger continued:

"Do not trouble the aristocrats and nobles. We do not want them to lose their homes. We have instituted laws for them and everyone else. Joshwa will tell you about it."

Joshwa cleared his throat.

"O people!" he said, and he began reading from scraps of paper: "First, all farmers, workers, builders, and miners are hereby exempt from personal income tax, which even the working slaves are forced to pay to the aristocrats, mobeds, and nobles."

A wave of joy rippled through the crowd.

"According to the constitution, the compulsory gifts demanded by mobeds on the occasions of Eid Nowruz, or the Persian New Year, and Mehregan, or the Persian Festival of Autumn, are hereby abolished."

The crowd was thunderstruck.

"All agrarian lands of the Sasanian empire previously owned by nobles shall be distributed equally among the people."

"Zindabad! Zindabad!" People jumped to their feet joyfully, chanting slogans. Joshwa was anxious. He was a Jew, and he had never seen his people so happy. They were in a state of constant fear lest they should fall out of favor with a king, vizier, elite, or

Zoroastrian mobed. For a moment, he was afraid that the ecstatic mob might attack him.

When he was leaving home, his father had said:

"Where are you off to, you fool! Jews only have Jews to turn to. These Aryans . . . you and I are at their mercy."

Had he been right?

Joshwa's heart quivered. His pupils dilated, and his throat went dry when the Aryan builders, farmers, craftsmen and miners sitting in front of him got to their feet, waving their arms ecstatically.

"Zindabad! Zindabad! Joshwa the Bookkeeper!"

Their slogans reverberated and surged in waves.

Joshwa was in a daze. What was happening here! He had never imagined anything like this. He was so elated that he couldn't even cry.

Outside Mazdak's haveli, mounted on a dark-almond-colored horse waiting in deference was Seyavash, with his small cavalry of a thousand warriors. Today, he was in the presence of the great commander-in-chief, but his ears and vigilant mind were preoccupied with his inner monologue. The commander-in-chief himself was waiting outside for the decisions being made that day.

"Be seated, be seated!" Mazdak's voice resonated.

The crowd took a few moments to settle down.

"From this day on, all fire temples in Ctesiphon are closed. Those of you who do not have homes may take shelter there. Three great fire temples in the city are enough. Their mobeds are required by law to learn farming or some other skill."

The crowd listened quietly. Joshwa had already finished one cup of water. His senses had recovered. He looked at the scribe, and said:

"Write it down! By order of the Messenger, a copy will remain in his safekeeping, and a copy each sent to all districts and judges of Ctesiphon."

The scribe spread out a fresh page on the three-legged stool before him and picked up his pen. He had brought this lightweight stool with him. Joshwa resumed reading off his scraps of paper:

"Annual income tax will now be paid by nobles and landowners instead of masons, builders, craftsmen, and miners. So far, they have always managed to avoid paying taxes by using one excuse or another. They claim that grain and fruit are perishable items, so how can they be taxed? By order of the Great Messenger and King of Kings, the Sovereign of the Sasanian Empire, taxes are hereby imposed on these items. All of you may keep your earnings in full. You are exempt from taxation. Farmers may keep one-sixth of their vegetables, fruits, and grain. Land taxes are as follows:

"One dirham annually on wheat and barley.

"Eight dirhams on grapes.

"Five dirhams on rice.

"Seven dirhams on fodder.

"Four dirhams on Persian date trees.

"Six dirhams on Aramean date trees.

"Six dirhams on olive trees."

Joshwa's voice was rising and falling. The scribe's pen plunged in and out of his inkpot. The rustle of pen on paper continued, like the gentle flutter of birds' wings.

The commander-in-chief entered at that very instant, parting the crowd.

"Stop for a moment," he said, bowing and offering salutations to the Messenger.

The scribe's pen ceased.

"What has been settled regarding military expenditures?" the commander demanded, struggling to maintain a respectful voice and tone. He wasn't used to that. He imagined that he was in a personal audience with the emperor.

"For battle?" the Messenger asked with mildly suppressed irritation. "No! The farmers and laborers won't pay a single dirham anymore. Gone are the days when their broken pots and vessels would be sold to cover war costs."

The commander-in-chief was quiet for a beat. Then he said:

"No . . . that's not what I meant. These farmers and such merely walk ahead of and behind the army. Their numbers are a sufficient contribution in battle. But will the *wuzurgan* and nobles volunteer their wealth for the royal treasury?"

"Write that down, too," Joshwa instructed the scribe. The scribe made note of it in his elaborate script.

"Approved," the Messenger nodded.

"Obliged, Great Messenger . . ." Shapur Mehran breathed a sigh of relief. As he turned to leave, the crowd scattered to make way for him, like scum dispersing on the surface of the water.

Mehran mounted his horse. His heart was calm now. He drew a sword from his scabbard and lifted it in the air: "Long live the Sasanian empire!" he roared. All soldiers in his cavalry raised their swords and chanted his slogan. The cavalry began a slow trot toward the streets of Ctesiphon.

Seyavash felt calm and content. Every soldier of the army was relieved. They had respect, honor, and they were paid a decent income on time. They were the warriors of the Sasanian empire.

Even Roman emperors feared them. Today, commander-in-chief Mehran had guaranteed their happiness. War was certain. If not today, then tomorrow.

With the Hunan nation? No. They were friends of the King. Qobad had spent a long time with them. Their emperor had once declared war against Qobad's father, King Peroz. The King was no match for their sudden and brutal attack, and the Sasanian army found itself surrounded. The mobeds that cursed Zarmeher's betrayal had weakened Peroz.

When Hunan's emperor, or the Great Khan, demanded a ransom, Peroz had been unable to pay it. It was then that they took little Qobad hostage. He lived in the Khan's palace for many years. After the first year or so, the Khan and his kind-hearted wife grew fond of Qobad. A few years later, when Peroz finally paid back the amount he owed, the Khan's eyes welled with tears as he bid Qobad farewell.

"I always knew that you would leave one day," said the emperor.

The empress did not make an appearance to say goodbye. She had been taken ill with sorrow.

"That is the magic of a child on a mother's heart . . . on the human heart!" his friend Mazdad used to say. Mazdad, now known as Mazdak—the Noble Messenger—had saved the beloved king's life by warning him, and had preserved Sasanid honor. These thoughts rippled through Seyavash's mind. At once, he began to miss his wife, children, and Mazdad.

What could he be doing? He must be praying to Geush Urwan, thought Seyavash.

* * *

The Prophet was reciting his prayers to Geush Urwan, invoking the soul of the sacred cow.

From an earthen cup, he poured a drop of fresh cow urine on a piece of scribbled paper. Now these were purified and consecrated ordinances.

The crowd sang a hymn. Then, they prostrated themselves before Mazdak. He did not stop them.

"O Ahura Mazda, he upon whom pours the light of the seven heavens, all spheres of the earth, and the human heart. You and I know that these people kneel before you, and only you," Mazdak called out. He felt aggrieved.

When the crowd lifted their heads from their gesture of gratitude, Mazdak said: "Henceforth, I am not your prophet. I am your *anduzgar*."

The crowd stared at him.

"What?" asked Barzin.

"*Anduzgar*. Meaning your teacher, your guru. The first and foremost difference between a prophet and a teacher is that you do not bow before your teacher. It offends Ahura Mazda."

Then, Mazdak asserted:

"We must bring about change. Major change. That is not easily done. We will organize into a group, and appoint a leader. We need to spread to the farthest corners of the Sasanian empire. Who is ready?"

Several youths quickly stepped forward. A few of them were not yet married, and were free from family obligations.

Barzin made his way through the crowd to the scribe sitting at the back.

"This message is the Supreme Messenger's final and absolute message. Spread the word throughout the entire kingdom. Tell them that the King and his army are with us."

But where must they go? deliberated Mazdak. "Take the message to the whole world," he commanded, changing his mind.

"Your name, give me your name," Barzin was asking the volunteers as the scribe jotted them down.

"The whole world!" a builder exclaimed. "But the people of Rum will kill us all."

"Then start with the Sasanid empire," advised Joshwa. "The Jewish laborers and workers will all join your cause."

Exactly how expansive and far-reaching is the Sasanid kingdom? Mazdak wondered, his forehead creasing. *Is it not the whole world? How foolish I have been . . . I never knew that Rum is not the only state under Sasanian rule.* Mazdak suddenly had the painful realization that he had been so absorbed in spiritual knowledge all his life that he practically had no worldly knowledge.

"The Sasanid empire?" blurted the scribe. "Where should I begin?"

Every curve and contour of the Sasanid empire was known to the scribe by heart. He had written rigorously about each province. All hopeful eyes were fixed upon him.

"We begin here—Faran, Kirman, Makran, Kuhistan, Parthia, Zabulistan, Margiana, Kushan, which is situated between River Jayhun and Sayhun, then Tukharistan, Sughd, and Khwas. Next, we come to Khuzd—Alban, Gharjistan, Azerbaijan, across the River Dujayl, and from Nusaybin to the Eastern shore of the Euphrates, and finally to Salukiyah, where . . ."

The scribe turned his head to look at Joshwa.

"Where followers of your faith reside in great numbers. Vast, sprawling temples. Then there's Babel, and Hirah here in Arabistan. They are all taxpaying communities. Even though they are not Zoroastrians, they will not harm the King's messengers," the scribe finished his thoughts.

"We shall go," said Kavus. His heart was beating wildly. "On camels, on horses, on oxcarts, on foot—by any means necessary."

"And . . . the women?" asked one farmer apprehensively.

"The women?" repeated Mazdak. He thought about it for a while.

"Are you married, farmer?" he asked.

"No, Messenger, my master, *anduzgar*. I don't have that kind of money," the farmer replied, his head lowered.

"I see," said Mazdak. "I'll let you know. Soon." Then, he got to his feet. "I am going inside. You should leave now."

The crowd slowly dispersed from the palace gates.

CHAPTER 16

A lone white cloud appeared in the clear Ctesiphon sky, and riding the air currents, sailed off into the distance. Along the shore of the River Tigris, countless farmers and laborers were gathered with eyes facing skyward, wistfully watching the cloud pass; the shade it cast was short-lived. The shore of the dried-up riverbed was crowded with people today. Barzin had led the crowd here. They all held shovels in their hands and were busy digging wells in different spots. Mazdak's eyes searched the crowd for Barzin.

"Honorable Prophet!" a mound of dirt called out to him. *Barzin?* Yes, it was Barzin. Mazdak walked over to the corner of the well. Barzin was covered in dirt. Half of his mud-covered torso was visible over the well. His face was caked with dirt, but his black eyes gleamed.

Mazdak observed the scene before him. His laborers were digging wells to pull up the water that was flowing down a slope.

"Three cubits!" a laborer called out, and another laborer quickly dug a tunnel at a height of three cubits—about the length of three forearms—and connected the two wells. At the edge of the shore, the wells were below sea level. The idea was that when the river filled these wells, a tunnel would direct this water to the other wells situated above sea-level. In this way, water would divert everywhere by its own force, ultimately reaching the gardens and fields around the cities.

Leaning his chest against the rim of the well, Barzin put his ear to the ground and listened intently. *Dhak, dhak, dhak* . . . as though a heart were throbbing beneath the dirt. It was the sound of a laborer's shovel in the neighboring well, digging a tunnel. If God willed it, they would hear the sound of water gushing into these tunnels. Soon . . . very soon.

"How can you be certain that it will rain soon here, and the water level of the Tigris will rise?" Mazdak asked. In the pit, white teeth flashed along with the black eyes.

"Many of us saw the sacred bull in the sky last night, noble Messenger . . . and . . . it bellowed twice, lord!"

"Oh!" Mazdak suddenly remembered—it was the month of *dozd*. Sixteen days had passed since his revelation. According to popular belief, the divine bull was destined to appear in the sky on the sixteenth night, its horns gilded with gold and its hoofs of silver. It would manifest only for a moment, and if it was fated to rain that year, it would bellow twice.

This was not written in the Avesta, but people had been perpetuating this belief for who knows how long. Mazdak smiled. Nevertheless, it did seem like it would rain. The special water of his motherland was sure to ascend through their underground mechanism. Mazdak woefully recalled the starving cattle whose pastures had dried up. *The grain in the warehouses will only last us until the next harvest,* he thought. *We need rain, or else we'll have to get our grain from the other provinces, and whether they like it or not is another matter entirely.*

"Your clothes have become sullied, holy prophet," Barzin said regretfully.

"Sullied? No, no . . ." answered Mazdak. His cloak and shalwar were stained with dirt. Mazdak touched it reverently. "This is sacred, too, Barzin . . . like fire, water, and air."

"Dirt is sacred!" Barzin repeated. The Prophet had already proclaimed it, but people were not yet fully convinced of its purity. They especially hesitated when invoking its name with fire. Fire, which was the epitome of holiness. But the Prophet clarified it with references from the Avesta:

"It is dirt that produces grain," he would teach them.

CHAPTER 17

That morning, all roads that led to Istakhr were blocked with chariots big and small. Caravans of the Sasanian elite flocked in from Khuzestan and Shiraz, from Isfahan, and from the faraway region of Kirman. Troubled aristocrats, anxious and fearful nobles, priests, and scribes, as well as numerous other members of the aristocracy were arriving from all over the kingdom. They had been invited here by Goshtasp. Even the Christian Jasaleeq of Salukiyah had devised a method to cross the Tigris and reach the city. The al-Majus, or Majusiyan, also arrived on their mules, decked out in red cloaks carrying their manuscripts. They had all come to attend the convention in the city that lay on River Pulvar, situated at some distance from Naqsh-e-Rostam, the oldest necropolis in the Sasanid kingdom. Istakhr's *attar*, or pure rose essence—pressed from fresh red roses—was renowned all over the world. The brocades produced here were used to tailor robes of honor for sultans, and the city's iron and mercury mines up in the mountains fulfilled the needs of the entire kingdom. But today, all miners had left work to come and listen to the message of the new prophet, Mazdak. Their eyes were fixed on the magnificent palaces and havelis. *Let all the wealth of the kingdom be distributed among its people equally. This is the message of Ahura Mazda*, was the word

Mazdak's followers were spreading. Was it possible? Indeed, news arriving from Ctesiphon indicated that it was already happening. Anduzgar Mazdak's disciples had reached the residents there and apprised them of his edict. They also reported that the message, bearing the King's special seal, had been delivered to all the city's judges.

Now what? Would they be able to get new clothes? Get their broken tools and weapons repaired? Would they be in a position to collect money for meher—the bride price—so they could marry? The message was official after all. But the judges were at a loss. None of them was prepared to answer these questions.

Istakhr was a hub of industry and handicraft, populated with artisans and craftspeople. Mazdak, too, rose to recognition from a little city called Madharaya in the province of Fars. This region had produced many great men. The influential historian Tansar's haveli was located here, and the city's library rivalled that of Ctesiphon's. Every evening, a festive air filled its lush gardens. At the edge of the city by a brook, Shahanshah Qobad had a little palace built for him, which was deserted these days. Qobad hadn't had the time to come and spend a few restful days here with his queen.

The small caravans of dignitaries went past the King's palace and thronged toward Goshtasp's sprawling haveli.

In the vestibule of the haveli, the straw curtains had been raised. The courtyard floor was covered by plush carpets lined with bolster pillows. Decorative sconces hung on the walls featuring the swastika pattern. The swastika was a symbol of Aryan courage, foresight, and affluence. The insignia was embroidered meticulously on the garment sleeves of the highest-ranking Sasanian army commanders. The swastika was depicted as two perpendicular lines in the shape of a cross, their arms bent at 90-degree angles, representing the revolving sun and the Wheel of Mithra, their sun god. As the guests came in, they bowed their heads at the sight of the swastika, and repeated: "Swast." *We are here, and the earth with all its wealth and treasures belongs to us!* Servants showered the visitors with roses. Their world hadn't changed just yet. Among the crowd of attendees were many distinguished names of the Sasanid empire, including Zoroastrian scholars such as Sipar Mahdad, Niv Shahpur, Wad Mazd, Azar Farrobag, Azar Buz, Azar Mehr, and Bakht Afrid. Dressed in a fine silk cloak, the chief mobed of Ctesiphon was also present. Mazdak had taken charge of his temple. The bishops of the two Christian sects in the kingdom were in attendance as well, both fearful of the Mazdakites. Of the two bishops, Baz Anis was also familiar with medicine, and had previously been appointed a royal physician. A storm of anger and despair raged in the hearts of everyone in the crowd, with each individual bursting to say their peace. But public etiquette posed a hindrance. All eyes were fixed on their host, Goshtasp.

Moving quickly through the preliminary formalities, Goshtasp faced the crowd and began speaking:

"Honored dignitaries, you are well aware that the province of Tabaristan, which has been under our reign for centuries since the decline of the Ashkanian empire, has lately been under attack by the Mazdakite uprising. Upon Qobad's son Kavus's arrival—whose mere mention offends my sensibilities—the farmers immediately revolted. Esteemed lords, they are breaking into our havelis, pillaging and plundering. They even . . ." his voice became hoarse. "They even dishonored our women."

The crowd gasped loudly. "Abominable!" shouts of protest were heard all round. "We have gathered here today to plan how to crush this wickedness and put an end to it." He turned to one of his servants: "Bring me a refreshing drink." The servant presented Goshtasp with sandalwood water in a gold cup. Other indentured servants offered drinks to the guests. The chief mobed dabbed his mouth with a handkerchief, and said:

"You know that we have always backed the nobles. We would have wrecked Qobad in a heartbeat, but it is our great misfortune that the commander-in-chief of the Sasanian army has joined their cause. They killed Zarmeher. You're the only one who can come up with a plan now."

Whispers rippled through the audience. Mehrdad mouthed, "Goshtasp is Qobad's worst enemy. As he should be."

"Why?" inquired the Christian bishop. He was new to this office and lived in Isbahan, quite a distance away from the capital city. Azar Mehr had once been an army officer. He whispered: "The thing is, the heaven-favored Zarmeher placed his greatest trust in Goshtasp. The pact that Goshtasp negotiated with the Armenians, our fellow believers, failed to put an end to the war. The conflict simply began anew. The Armenians had already defeated Qobad's cavalry last year. Goshtasp is accused of accepting a chestful of treasure from the Armenians in exchange for signing the peace treaty. God knows the truth of the matter," he finished, stroking his beard.

The people in the crowd were engaged in a heated debate. It had started raining again. The straw curtains in the courtyard were lowered once more. The servants lit lanterns and chandeliers with candles. The congregation attendees seethed with fury. *Qobad, Qobad! It was an ill-fated hour when we put his name forward for kingship!*

"Shall we seek help from the *hawanan* of Caucasus?"

"Or ask the Kurayshis for support?"

"The Tanukh tribes of Hirah?"

"Nobody can be entrusted with this message," replied Goshtasp. "These are dangerous times. We will have to rely on our sons."

Their sons were seated nearby. Mehrdad's son was listening intently to his father.

"Baba! I am ever at your command," he pledged.

Outside, the rain poured harder.

CHAPTER 18

There was no sign of unrest in Tabaristan.

Upon his arrival, the residents welcomed Prince Kavus exuberantly. A sea of humble farmers and laborers received him with eager affection. Kavus had not only delivered Mazdak's message to all the officials, but also the new scheme of land allotment according to the royal edict, which was being enforced across the province. "All hail the Sasanid empire! Long live Qobad, King of Kings!" the cities and villages of Tabaristan reverberated with these slogans. The treasury of the province, which had been transferred into the Goshtasp family's private coffers under their reign, was now adequately abundant. The King's new tax policy seemed tolerable to everyone. This province was especially dear to Qobad, where oranges, wheat, and rice were grown in plenitude, and which was home to great mountain ranges like Mount Damavand. Mount Damavand, the towering summit fabled to have been the home of the Simurgh, the mythical bird. Both Qobad and his king-wife Naindokht loved the silks of Tabaristan. The Tabaristani people had procured silkworms from Khita and brought them back to Tabaristan, where they now produced their own fabric. Bolts of suti, a type of cotton, were loaded on camels traveling with trade caravans across the kingdom's thoroughfares. The demand for cotton was booming because the lower classes were buying clothes now. Half-clad weavers, who for centuries had been manufacturing yarn in their little cottages made out of wood and reeds, were buying new garments for themselves.

Qobad had not been able to visit here for a long, long time, because Goshtasp's family was from Tabaristan and the region had been quite self-sufficient under his rule, and the chief priest was Goshtasp's loyalist. "I wish to appoint Kavus as the Shah of Tabaristan, Wise Messenger," he said to Mazdak. "His presence has inspired fealty for the King and the Sasanian kingdom in the hearts of the people. They are impressed with his sagacity."

Mazdak pondered over this. The truth was that he preferred Kavus's presence in Ctesiphon. He had been very attentive to the prince's upbringing for some time now. But he conceded, "As you wish, Your Majesty."

The delay in Mazdak's reply had discomfited the King. "I need your advice and consent," he said. After many years, he was finally rid of the nobles—the *wuzurgan*, *dabiran*, and *mobedan*—who had always imposed their will upon him. The King was no more than a prisoner or puppet to them. Would Prophet Mazdak restrict his discretions too, he wondered skeptically. Why was he not readily bowing his head in agreement and admiring his wisdom?

The tie between the King and a prophet of God is tenuous. It is only by supporting each other that they have a hope of getting along, thought Qobad.

His doubts soon proved unwarranted.

"You know the affairs of the Sasanian state best, my king," Mazdak replied with deference.

The King smiled. He was sitting in a shady nook of the palace garden with Mazdak and a few of his companions. The wilted grass had been covered with carpets on account of the drought. Qobad's heart felt content. He wanted to discuss the defense of Nusaybin with his commander-in-chief.

"Summon Shapur Mehran," he ordered his servant.

Shapur Mehran was standing before his troops in a wide field beside his haveli. Brightly colored flags of the Sasanian troops fluttered in the breeze—the Kayanian army, the Gundeshapurian army—the Sasanian cavalry was comprised of hundreds of such troops where the cavalry as well as infantry were conscripted from the same family. He had just given a new idea to his Hazar Pati commanders—the generals with one thousand men under their command.

Not long ago at the royal palace, he had observed a troupe of performers. Each dancer lifted their feet and arms in perfect synchrony with the rest of the troupe. "If the army were to move the same way," Shapur proposed to his troops, "but not like performers," he added with a grimace, "your movements should be the picture of wrath and fury."

"Bring your right arm forward in a single explosive motion," he ordered.

The cavalry complied.

"Withdraw arm!" he commanded. As he shouted instructions, Shapur Mehran demonstrated with precise movements of his own body.

"Now lift your right arm and right leg. All together!" he bellowed. "Next, lift your left arm and left leg in one swift movement," he ordered, and strode forward in demonstration.

The troops followed, marching onward.

Shapur Mehran rubbed his hands in triumph.

A formidable sight lay before him. Thousands of soldiers marched in a single formation, like a mob moving in an orderly but grim fashion. It was a mob that would be impossible for ordinary men to overpower.

"Turn your faces to the right!" he whipped his neck around. In the distance, an elderly woman was gathering wood in the withered grass near a copse of bushes. She raised her head. As soon as her eyes locked with the commander general of the Sasanian army, she ran off.

The royal musicians sounded their drums. A tambourinist lifted his tambourine and began playing a steady, propulsive beat. Soon, the musicians were strumming a tune in unison with the sounds of the army's rising and falling feet. It was a synchronous, awe-inspiring rhythm.

"Excellent! Excellent!" Shapur Mehran rejoiced at the success of his inventive idea.

Upon receiving the King's message, he designated a Hazar Pati to supervise the army in his absence. Then, he mounted his horse and rode off in the direction of the palace.

"Our troops are ready to face the Roman army, Your Highness," he submitted to Qobad. Then, he added with some hesitation: "I have even taught them how to march in unison. The enemy will take one look at our charging troops and tremble with fear."

Qobad beamed.

"A messenger broke this news to us just before you arrived. He even gave a quick demonstration."

"Very good!" Shapur Mehran smiled respectfully. He suddenly remembered the old woman collecting wood. *The King's secret network of spies is on the alert,* he thought contentedly.

"Shapur, we have heard that the Roman cavalry is performing similar parades on the highways, while onlookers shower them with flower petals."

The news came as a surprise to Shapur Mehran. "Is that so?" he asked. "That only proves that we are their equals in every way."

Mazdak contemplated this in silence. There wasn't a more unnatural manner for man to walk upon Ahura Mazda's beautiful, verdant earth. The glorious, esteemed Maker did not create man to walk in such a fashion. But Mazdak did not want to provoke debate. Whenever he had an opinion, he would relay it to his treasured friend Seyavash, who was like a bridge between Mazdak and Qobad. He had no interest in how the troops should or shouldn't march. *They can do as they please*, he thought.

Qobad and the commander general awaited Mazdak's response with hopeful eyes.

"The army can march however they please," he replied in a bittersweet tone. "As long as they protect us and the Sasanid empire."

His answer satisfied Shapur Mehran. Getting down on his knees, he made obeisance to Mazdak. *He is a noble prophet in every way*, he thought to himself.

Feeling victorious, the commander made his exit from the palace.

CHAPTER 19

"A flawless face, fair skin that glows like the moon."

Dipping his pen in a pot of green ink, Narsi the scribe composed his words eagerly. He was writing on a long, silken ream of Phoenician paper that had just arrived. In the margins, an artist had painted a beautiful rose vine with green and red ink. The paper was fragrant with the scent of *attar*. Narsi sat beneath an arched window at the library, his legs folded under him. The shutters were open, letting the faint perfume of spring blossoms in. He looked out for a moment, then returned to his writing.

"Soft, exquisite skin, big, dark eyes, a high nose, fine eyebrows, high cheekbones, pleasing stature, thick, ebony locks, a wide forehead, beautifully-shaped ears, an elegant, swan-like neck, ample, firm breasts." Narsi was copying a letter sent by Munzir, the ruler of Hirah, along with a handmaid as a gift for King Qobad. In his letter, he had detailed her many admirable qualities. Qobad's face broke into a smile when he read the letter. He ordered that the letter be preserved in the royal *divan*. The epistle was read aloud in his private court, and his courtiers were most entertained. "By God, this should be considered the very ideal of beauty," remarked one of them. All agreed.

Now, as he copied the contents of the letter, thin, scrawny Narsi felt more and more overwrought at each line.

"Supple shoulders, dainty wrists, and soft palms with long, slender fingers. An enchanting figure with a narrow waist and delicate modesty; her hips are full, her thighs shapely. Defined ankles and taut calves, rippling beneath her anklets. She walks with measured grace, each stride winning the hearts of the courtiers. Obedient to her lord, honorable, with a quiet and gentle disposition. Born of a respectable family, she lives harmoniously with kin and exercises sound judgment in all matters. Her saliva is sweet as nectar, and her very presence brings radiance to the household. Should it please Your Majesty to summon her to your bed, she will welcome you with warmth. Yet, if Your Majesty does not desire her, she will withdraw with grace. Searching eyes that linger on you, cheeks flushed, rose-colored lips—the embodiment of love—forever eager to come to you."

Narsi sighed deeply as he rolled up the scroll. Once more, his eyes wandered outside the window, where the azure sky appeared tangled up with the manicured hedges at the far end of the garden. Beyond the window, he saw the handmaiden clearly. Holding the tip of his pen lightly between his lips—an anchor for his swirling thoughts—Narsi imagined himself putting on different kinds of clothes of his liking on the handmaiden and then taking them off.

Observing the motion of his hands under the shawl, a scribe sitting close by nudged Narsi:

"What were you writing?"

Narsi snapped out of his reverie and extended his scroll to the scribe.

"Portrait of a fairy-like beauty!" he exclaimed, laughing heartily. "I envy your luck, my friend! We only get to write petty receipts for them." The scribe skimmed through the description. Then, he asked:

"Is this regarding the handmaiden from Hirah? Has the King accepted then?"

"With utmost pleasure . . ." said Narsi, "but probably not for himself. He is simply enamored with his queen, who is just as beautiful."

"For Prince Kavus then?"

"Perhaps . . ." replied Narsi, "but Kavus is hardly here anymore. He's wandering around in other provinces, spreading Mazdak's message. He took three horses. He means to ride each of them, one after the other."

"Do you think the queen is like her?" the scribe whispered. "Wouldn't the manual labor she did as a child have hardened her palms?"

Even though people made every effort to keep it under wraps and nobody spoke of it publicly, the whole kingdom knew the queen's story. Queen Naindokht was not of royal blood. She was a memory from one of Qobad's hunting expeditions in his youth. The daughter of a farmer from a remote village by the jungle, she had captured the young king's heart as soon as he set eyes upon her. She had been fourteen or fifteen years old at the time, milking cows for the hunters. Qobad settled the matter with the farmer then and there, and brought her to the royal palace with him, where all the wedding rituals were performed. Khosrow, Qobad's younger son, was from Queen Naindokht. The older son Kavus's mother belonged to a royal family. A few short years after Qobad's second wedding, she passed on from the mortal world. Hence,

Naindokht became the Sasanian monarch's king-wife and queen of the Sasanian empire. Her beauty was sublime, and when she accompanied King Qobad on a tour of the kingdom in the royal carriage, dressed all in white and wearing a crown of iridescent white pearls, people were awestruck.

"Hm!" The scribe finished reading the letter and took a deep breath. "This unearthly beauty could also be the imagination of Hirah's scribe at work."

"No!" chewing on his nails, Narsi wheeled around. He sighed. "You're just being skeptical. She's sure to be exactly the way she has been described."

"Hm!" the other scribe smiled. Then, he said: "Hundreds of such goddesses have been recovered from the very havelis of Ctesiphon. O Narsi! Do not invite a heinous death upon yourself by coveting the King's handmaiden. There are many others out there . . . but they are usually grabbed by farmers and peasants. As for us, we are left empty-handed! Narsi, you have been tasked with recording Mazdak's sayings. Why don't you get one for yourself? And put in a good word for the rest of us, too."

"Taking someone by force is beyond the capability of us scribes. On the other hand, if a law were to be passed, that would be a different story," answered Narsi. "But . . ." he said with obvious disappointment, "the Prophet has not yet ordained any law regarding women."

"They say he'll do it in the next sitting," the scribe ventured.

"Yes . . . or they'll send us the edict . . . we are all waiting in anticipation."

Dastarkhwan had been laid out in the library. Two or three other scribes joined Narsi in his room. And what was for supper? Vegetable mash, yogurt, and naan as usual. They had given up all hope of eating meat. The Prophet had condemned it. *Why take other lives to fill our bellies and satisfy our appetites for flavor?* Mazdak provoked. Word on the street was that even the King had stopped eating meat.

"There is news of rain from Fars. Will the clouds ever reach us in Ctesiphon?" Rumors were going around in the streets and alleys of the empire's capital.

Mazdak had planned on departing from his haveli early in the morning, but he ran into Yaqutdokht waiting at his door.

"My lord . . ." she said softly.

Mazdak looked at her with raised eyebrows.

"I'm getting married, lord . . ."

Mazdak was taken aback.

"Married? To whom?" he asked after a momentary pause.

"To your gardener," Yaqutdokht dropped her gaze and replied.

"The gardener! Ahvaz?" Mazdak inquired. The news was so sudden that he was at a loss for words. He took a few moments to compose himself, then said:

"Very well. Does Ahvaz have money for the bride price?"

"Yes, lord. He sold a carpet that he received in his share from the raids."

"Hm . . ." Mazdak pondered over this. Marriage without the bride price wasn't permissible, and Mazdak was not one to eschew the principles of religion—although he was in the midst of establishing a few new ones.

"Very well. Send for your parents . . ." Mazdak advised as he stepped out of his room. "I will arrange your marriage. You were my subordinate wife, Yaqutdokht. Today, I free you."

Just two days ago, Bamdad had asked Mazdak: "Shall we arrange another woman for you?" Mazdak now realized why his father had asked him that question. *Baba must have known she was about to leave*, he thought. Time and again, Mazdak had refused his father's persistent offer: "I already have a wife. One is enough." In reply, Bamdad would sigh and fall silent. He wanted to see his bloodline flourish during his lifetime.

Yaqutdokht's news made Mazdak think. He went back into his room and sat down on the carpet, his legs folded beneath him. Opening the drawer of a small table, he pulled out a pen, ink, and paper, and began writing:

"All subordinate wives of the aristocracy are hereby released. They shall be distributed to those among the poor who remained unmarried because they could never afford the bride price. The bride price is officially set at one dirham. For those who cannot afford even a dirham, their bride price shall be paid from the royal coffers."

Narsi wept bitterly as he wrote down the edict. He already had a wife, so he did not have a rightful claim over another maiden.

"This is sheer brutality," he said placing a hand over his heart. "It is unnatural!"

"For hundreds of years, Aryan men have enjoyed multiple women at a time. Prophet Mazdak . . . the messenger . . . maybe he is impotent."

"Why?" Narsi's wife asked with an amused smile. She had washed and changed their seven children, and now settled for the night with her sewing basket open in front of her. They were expecting their eighth child soon, and she was making quilts in preparation.

"What the Holy Prophet Mazdak is saying is absolutely right. I approve of his message. Why, Narsi . . ." she waved her hand and asked, "why don't we women have a few subordinate husbands in addition to our main one? You men are always telling us that one husband is enough for us. Then why is one wife not enough for you men?"

"Damn Mazdak is an idealist," grumbled Narsi, biting his nails. "He's out of touch with reality."

The vision of that ideal of feminine beauty had vanished from before his eyes now. To Narsi's mind, that vision had inspired a fellow Arab scribe's imagination, and it was so close to reality that it was present within the walls of the royal palace right at that moment, and was being discovered in the havelis of Ctesiphon every day.

"An idealist! Come now, he's a prophet. What else could he be? No, we women support him wholeheartedly. Long live Prophet Mazdak!"

"Silence!" Narsi scolded his wife. "It's not like they take you to public gatherings or anything."

But he knew his wife was the daughter of a scribe, and very well-educated. She usually finished all the work that he brought home from the library. He didn't want to displease her, but he was irritated. Anyhow, he had to leave for work now.

"You give women away as gifts. Have you ever asked them if they like someone? You act as if they have no feelings. You shove four dirhams into their hands each month, and expect them not to ask for a single dirham more than that. That is tyranny, anarchy, injustice."

His wife went on talking.

Narsi looked at her dejectedly. *Women have no sense*, he thought. *The adage is true. But the saying that they are voiceless! Any husband knows that's completely false. Alas, it's the opposite!*

* * *

Mazdak, who had once been Mazdad, was not impotent.

When he first laid eyes on Naindokht, it was as if his eyes had been struck by a bolt of lightning. Naindokht had come with her son to pay homage to Mazdak. She did not enter the room. Rather, she breezed straight into his heart. Just before the fleeting moment dissipated, Mazdak imagined the queen in his arms. He felt a deep longing for her stir within his body and soul. He was a gentle, warm person who liked to keep his own counsel. Mazdak couldn't articulate his feelings, but his eyes orbited her every movement.

On their way back, Khosrow asked: "Mother, why was the Prophet looking at you like that?"

Naindokht panicked. *Children see and understand everything. Nosherwan, my son, he's not a little boy anymore*, she thought.

"Shh!" she hushed him. "Don't mention it to anyone!"

Should I tell my husband, she wondered. *But what will I say? That there was something in the way he looked at me? In his eyes? No.*

She was hopelessly in love with Qobad, who had whisked her away from the village and brought her to his palace. Where she had initially felt like a stranger . . . where she would often hide and cry because she missed her mother. But Qobad's charms had won her over. In his arms, she had blossomed into a woman, and then she had fallen for this brave, noble man. Back home, most of the girls her age had a similar story.

This shall remain a secret between prophet and queen, she resolved, and taking hold of her son's hand, she kept walking.

CHAPTER 20

There were two of them. Leaving their horses behind in a caravanserai at Hirah, they rode on camels toward the south of the city. It had taken them two days to get to Hirah. If they had taken the shortcut, they would have risked the danger of being recognized. Outside the city limits, they saw the earth changing. They were riding in the desert now, and the endless expanse of sand left no clear demarcation of where the desert began or ended. They would surely have been lost by now if it weren't for their camel-herder, racing ahead effortlessly on bare feet, the camel's reins gripped tightly in his hands. He had an instinctive grasp of the landscape—which was barely perceptible to the young Sasanian riders—as if discerning it by magic. Instead of swirling with the hot air currents, the coarse sand shifted beneath their feet so swiftly that a cliff that was right ahead of them disappeared from view momentarily, then suddenly loomed above them on their left.

Dadar had brought Mehrdad along because he was familiar with the Arabic language. His ancestors might very well have been Arabs, nobody could say for sure. Centuries ago, Arabs had attacked and invaded Istakhr. Some left after the raids, but many stayed behind—Ashkanian wealth suited them. They married

Persian beauties, and now, it was nearly impossible to distinguish them from the natives. Thus, the Arabic language was no stranger to such families in Istakhr.

"Water! Water!" said Dadar. He cupped his hands and gestured towards his mouth, signaling the camel-herder.

"Not much farther," the camel-herder said as he untied the waterskin bag from his waist and threw it to the riders. Mehrdad leaped towards it and caught it.

"What did he say?" Dadar gulped down some water and asked.

"He says we don't have far to go," Mehrdad repeated.

A short distance away, a patch of green shimmered into view. An oasis! The closer they got to the grove of lofty date palms, the wider Dadar's eyes became.

"God alone knows how such fertile black soil thrives in the middle of a barren, lifeless stretch of sand!" he exclaimed.

A range of rocky mountains arose on their right. The winds suddenly calmed. The gurgling sounds of a brook resembled a sweet melody that delighted their ears. Encampments of the Tanukhid tribe spread out before them.

Abu Abbas was waiting for them. He had already received word of their arrival. A rug had been laid out in front of his tent. He rose to welcome the travelers. He was a tall, dark-skinned, lean, middle-aged Bedouin. His eyes glittered beneath thick, dark eyebrows.

Mehrdad and Dadar quickly cut to the chase.

"Attack! Launch an attack on our kingdom immediately . . ."

Abu Abbas listened to them quietly. His ears honed in on every word of their conversation, while his gaze, occasionally cast downward, examined every nuance of emotion on the visitors' faces. *Is this a trap?* was his first thought. He studied the manner in which both Aryans sat on his carpet. The precise moment they shifted onto their side, and why. The specific matter that caused them to hunch their shoulders and lean forward.

Finally, he spoke:

"May Al-Uzza shower you with grace. Why do you wish for us to plunder your kingdom?"

"Tell him to forget about that, Mehrdad . . . we will supply the weapons . . . and we will also give them horses," Dadar interjected impatiently.

Mehrdad scratched his head.

"That won't work," he replied in a voice barely above a whisper. "You don't know these Bedouins, Dadar. They won't make a single move until they get to the heart of the matter. There's no alternative but to tell them the truth."

"Abu Abbas! The Sasanian empire has been taken over by imposters. We want to reclaim our government."

"Who wants to?" Abu Abbas asked.

"My father, and . . . my uncle . . ." Mehrdad replied helplessly.

"Ah!" Abu Abbas tilted his head. "So, it is your father and uncle's government that has been toppled?" he asked as understanding dawned on him.

He was the leader of the Tanukhids, who were his tribesmen. But tribes were comprised of castes, which in turn consisted of multiple family units. Maternal uncles, paternal uncles, brothers. Their respect, their honor—it was their nucleus. A Bedouin could lay down his life for them, and could take a life just as easily.

"Tell him that a man over there wants to seize the wealth of the nobility and distribute it among everyone," Dadar elbowed Mehrdad.

"That would be futile," Mehrdad shook his head. "He is convinced that even he has a claim over the nobility's wealth, which is the whole reason they raid the trade caravans in the first place."

"Hm!" Abu Abbas gave his sons a knowing look. They promptly stood up and headed towards the grove of date palms.

"We have raided your kingdom several times." Abu Abbas said to the Aryans. "But your king and our leader Malik Munzir have become good friends. Since then, we have ceased our attacks in your region, and are now targeting the Ghassanid caravans."

"Will Munzir try to dissuade you?" Mehrdad asked curiously.

"Dissuade us?" Abu Abbas repeated, an expression of disbelief on his face. Then, he burst out laughing. "He wields no influence over us. We are free men, stranger," he brandished a slender arm in the air.

"Then go, and kill every single child in Ctesiphon," Mehrdad said fiercely.

"Wait," said Abu Abbas. "I believe you've misunderstood. This sword," he gestured to the leather sheath tied to his long cloak, "is raised only when our life is in danger. We do not kill for sport—whether lance, spear, or sword, these are only used as our last resort. They will have to attack us first."

"Make them your prisoners, and slaughter them as sacrificial offerings in the name of Goddess Uzza," Mehrdad spurred Abu Abbas. He knew about the Arab ritual of making human sacrifices to the deity.

A smile played on Abu Abbas's lips. "Goddess Uzza does not accept offerings of non-Arabs! That's why we grab Ghassanid children."

Abu Abbas's sons returned balancing huge iron platters laden with freshly barbequed, succulent pieces of lamb meat atop their heads. In honor of the visitors, the host had just slaughtered a well-fed, prime lamb. A few moments later, the ground beneath the open skies was covered by rugs, as if they had appeared out of thin air. Around fifteen to twenty people had been invited to the feast. They brought pitchers of milk, date halwa, long-necked earthen flasks filled with olive oil, and pickled olives with them.

The Arabs were mingling with each other. The defensive wall of Ctesiphon's fortress was exceptionally sturdy. The Aryans had fortified it with such precision that it was impregnable. But the westward bend in River Tigris left the lower side of the wall relatively weaker. The wall was flanked on both sides by marshy land, which meant that military troops rarely took that route. It wouldn't be hard to make a hole in the wall. Bags of gleaming Sasanian coins were being delivered to their tents.

The Arab poet dabbed his face with a handkerchief, and in a mellifluous voice, started singing:

O Uzza! Divine mother of earth and sky!
Have mercy upon me,
and on my brother —
O queen of the world!
Pour your grace upon us,
But upon no one else.

The Bedouin celebration was alive with laughter. They lavished praise upon the poet, their arms spread wide. Poets were the light of the Bedouins' eyes. The sons of Hirah spent years serving poets in their tents to learn from them and master the Arabic language. *How unfortunate that our language is beyond the comprehension of these non-Arabs. Poor souls!* they thought. It was Uzza's will that all creation be denied this miracle of eloquence—save for them. *It is as if they are deaf and mute!* they surmised, taking pity on them.

This was the last lamb in Abu Abbas's household. *We will have to survive on the bare minimum until the next raid*, Abu Abbas thought grimly. *So be it. Anything for our guests—anything.*

CHAPTER 21

"These Aryans . . . they insist on calling themselves Aryan, but they haven't acted like Aryans for a long time now."

Joshwa's teacher was in conversation with him. He had been sick for many days now, and good, kind Joshwa had come to pay him a visit. His teacher was propped up in bed, supported by pillows. He was telling his bright student all those things that he spent day and night scribbling on scraps of fine vellum. "History . . . I have a written record of history," he rasped. The faint odor of leather lingered in his room.

"It must be preserved, dear Master," said Joshwa. He surveyed the room, where countless scrolls of vellum were stuffed haphazardly into recesses in the walls, collecting dust.

"Preserved!" the old teacher sighed. "Does anything remain preserved in this world? It will survive . . . as long as a foreign army doesn't set fire to the city and burn everything in it . . . but I know. I have spent my whole life on this research."

"The Elamites were the first ones to settle here. Dusky Elamites," he said, his finger drawing pictures in the air. "They intermingled with the Aryans—same old story—men and women forging bonds. Then came the Khotani people. Next were the Arabs, who came and went intermittently. And don't get me started on the Greeks, ogling and lusting after women. They, too, were fraternizing with the Aryans. So I ask: what Aryans are they talking about? Jews are the last remaining pure bloodline, my son."

"The Elamites live on to this day. Most of them are fisherfolk," said Joshwa.

"Indeed. Some are lost to assimilation, while others endure." The master rolled over on his other side. "Happens every time, or so they say."

Once again, his finger traced something in the air. "A long time ago, thousands of years ago . . . many Elamites left for Hind with their idols and statues."

Then, he added with certainty: "It is us, and only us, the descendants of Abraham, who have preserved their bloodline."

"Twelve tribes," Joshwa replied wearily, "no one may join our ranks, nor can we join another."

Even as he coughed, the old man let out a laugh: "And yet, you have joined the Aryans . . . who likely believe that shaking your hand absolves them."

"They are fond of me, Master. Because I concern myself not only with my son and my tribe, but with the well-being of all people. Ctesiphon's working class consists of the impoverished from tribes all over the world. People come here from distant lands to find labor. To a laborer, what meaning do land or lineage hold, Master?"

Joshwa wanted to leave now. He often felt uneasy, sensing that other Jews resented his popularity in Ctesiphon. "What have you ever done for us Jews?" their accusatory eyes seemed to ask.

He took his leave and set out for his Aryan friend's house. Danazad had been a schoolteacher like him. He had passed away, leaving Joshwa heartbroken. He was going to offer his condolences to Danazad's wife and children. Danazad, much like Joshwa, had fervently advocated for Mazdak's cause. *I lost my dear friend to a common fever*, Joshwa thought with regret.

Grief clung to the house. Danazad's wife sat with her head bowed in sorrow. It was Joshwa's first time in this house. A house of mourning offers no hospitality. He had a simple glass of water and left. At the door, he caught sight of a little girl. She must have been seven or eight years old.

"*Adaab*," the girl lowered her head addressed Joshwa.

"Is it Danadokht? Danazad's daughter?"

"Yes, uncle." The girl studied Joshwa carefully—his dark hair, broad forehead, and his pitch-black, bright, intelligent eyes.

Joshwa drew out a dirham from his pocket and placed it on her hand.

"Treat yourself to some sweets, Danadokht."

"No!" she blurted out. "I'll give it to Prophet Mazdak."

"Ah, so you've heard of Prophet Mazdak!"

"Yes! My father used to tell me about him," she replied.

She ran off into the street, where her friends were beckoning at her to come and play with them. She turned around one last time to look at Joshwa, then disappeared in the crowded street.

Joshwa never went back, nor did he ever see the little girl again. *Danazad's family name had once been Kamboch*, Joshwa mused on his way. There had been a scribe by the name of Shah Kamboch . . . but with the passage of time, the differences between tribes had all but disappeared. All tribes had scattered across the earth in search of livelihoods. *Master was right*, thought Joshwa. *Not a single bloodline remains pure.*

CHAPTER 22

In just two days, Shapur Mehran's cavalry had apprehended three Jews and cast them at his feet. They captured them in Salukiyah, across the River Tigris. Some of their men had disguised themselves as women and infiltrated a Jewish settlement under the pretense of seeking work. They had gained access to a haveli where the Jewish representative was plotting to establish a sovereign Jewish state. The three Jews, too, listened in as the details of the plot were revealed. Shapur's men had no trouble identifying them, as they served in the Jewish division of the Sasanian army. When the gathering broke up, the soldiers followed them and launched their attack.

"Throw them in jail," ordered the commander-in-chief. He wanted to expose this conspiracy to the King without wasting any time.

After lunch, Shapur Mehran requested the King's permission and promptly arrived in his private chambers. Qobad was in conversation with his middle son Khosrow, Prophet Mazdak, and Seyavash. They were discussing important affairs of state.

When Shapur Mehran had finished, the King grew pensive. *So that's what the Jewish leaders are plotting.* He reasoned that these aspirations of freedom were hardly unusual for an empire of such grandeur, where several factions had previously attempted to assert their autonomy. But these conspiratorial designs had to be suppressed—a task the formidable Sasanid cavalry carried out with unparalleled skill. He gave Khosrow a meaningful glance, as if to say: "My dearest son, both kinsmen and strangers alike will seek to usurp your inheritance."

Khosrow answered his father's questioning eyes with silence, and lowered his gaze in deference. His eyes burned with resolve and intent. Reassured, Qobad turned toward his commander-in-chief.

"To deal with the traitorous Jews of Salukiyah, ten cohorts of your feared army will more than suffice. But it is essential that they be made a warning to all, to ensure that none henceforth dares threaten the Sasanian crown."

Shapur placed a hand on his chest and bowed.

"If it pleases you, my sovereign, I shall have them sentenced to death as our most reviled criminals are—by hammering nails into their flesh."

Mazdak had been listening quietly to the entire conversation. At the commander-in-chief's words, his face went suddenly pale. His dark eyes flitted about like those of a wounded pigeon.

"No . . . n . . . no . . ." he stuttered, his voice faltering.

"Not torture . . ." he pushed himself up from the carpet, steadying himself with one hand. "Do not torment a living soul . . . every scream out of their mouth will rend the heavens above. We will be doing Ahriman's work . . . let no living being be tortured."

Qobad watched him closely. This man, who now called himself a prophet, was his savior. Even now, as his subjects ransacked palaces and havelis, hurling abuses at nobles and priests alike, the King's own palace stood safe. Outside its walls, the people still sang his praises. Qobad had grown fond of Mazdak. Seyavash couldn't restrain himself—*Don't be absurd*—these words burned at the tip of his tongue, but he bit them back.

"Honorable Prophet . . . what is it you truly want? First you oppose the death penalty. Now, you speak against torture. Then how are we to carry out punishments?"

Mazdak was quiet for a while. Then, he said: "Imprisonment alone is a grave punishment. At least give this a chance. Let it be known that, henceforth, under your merciful reign, prisoners shall be tortured no more."

Every person in the room fell silent. These men were seasoned in such matters, and each was lost in thought. Only young Khosrow wore an expression of thinly veiled contempt. He bit his lip, his head bowed. When the meeting came to an end and Qobad instructed him to kneel before the Prophet, Khosrow pressed a hand on his forehead, and said:

"I have a terrible headache, Your Highness."

At once, Qobad's face clouded with worry. The King loved his son dearly. He was handsome, dutiful, and the coolness of his eyes. Born of his beloved queen, the boy was a symbol of the love had taken root in his heart the moment he laid eyes on her.

"Oh! What's wrong? Shall I send for the physician Borzuya?"

"With your permission, may I rest for a while?" Khosrow requested, a hand over his chest.

"Of course," replied Qobad.

The prince took his leave.

Seyavash left for home alongside Mazdak.

"Mazdad!" he said. "Prince Khosrow doesn't like you,"

"Hm . . ." said Mazdak. "In the end, my dear friend, the All-good Spirit will overcome the Foul One!"

Seyavash smiled weakly in reply. He drew back the baize curtain of his chariot window and watched the barren land outside the palace blur past. He did not believe for a moment that Mazdad, now called Prophet Mazdak, was truly a prophet. Mani, Seyavash thought, *Perhaps Mani had been one . . .* He had been executed long ago. Only someone whose life had vanished into the distant past could wear the halo of prophethood. *A man who walks among us, who breathes among us, how can one believe such a man to be a prophet!* He smiled to himself. Like many in Ctesiphon, Seyavash saw Mazdak as no more than a reformer. And reform? In truth, the results weren't bad. His eyes roved around the land stretching outside the palace walls. Once, these grounds had crawled with starving mobs bleating like animals. Now, not a single beggar could be seen. While the famine still went on, the poor at least received their daily porridge of barley and wheat twice a day. No more news came of anyone dying a slow, wretched death for want of food. But death by illness? *That*, Seyavash thought, *was Ahura Mazda's will.*

"When justice prevails, there will neither be crime nor war," Mazdad's words echoed in his mind.

That remains to be seen, Seyavash thought, shaking his head. His spies had just delivered news of the Jewish mutiny in Salukiyah.

War was inevitable.

CHAPTER 23

"Why . . . Abba . . . why?"

Joshwa sat in his father's library, his legs folded beneath him. "Why do we seek to break ourselves from the Sasanian crown, to bring it to ruin?" he implored.

In the pale glow of the lantern, his father was hunched over a book. He looked up at Joshwa, then returned to his reading.

But Joshwa wanted an answer.

"What haven't the Iranians done for us?" He pressed. "You're the one who, ever since I was a child, taught me our history. For eight hundred years, we Jews have lived in peace among the Aryans. Ever since Nebuchadnezzar exiled us from Jerusalem. Ever since the Romans destroyed the Temple of Solomon."

Joshwa paused to take a breath. He studied his father carefully. The yellow lamplight flickered across his features, casting shadows on his face. His aging, wrinkled face was motionless, and it seemed as though his eyes were closed.

Joshwa strained to recall something—anything—that might stir his father's memory. "King Kourosh gave us refuge. He allowed us to return to Jerusalem and rebuild Solomon's Temple. With his support, the Jews succeeded."

"It was never finished . . . we were one arch short."

"The Parthians took care of us too, Abba," Joshwa continued. "They appointed a high-ranking official among us. They gave him the title of *Resh Galut*. He is our spiritual guide. He settles our disputes. We Jews live in the Sasanian kingdom by the commandment of Prophet Musa, Abba."

Joshwa was talking to his father in Pahlavi—the Middle Persian language. He had almost completely forgotten the Hebrew language.

His father turned to look at him.

"We Jews have given our lives as soldiers in the armies of the Arya empire, my son. We shed our own blood to build this state."

Joshwa held his ground.

"For centuries, we have collected interest and taxes on their behalf. In return for our military and non-military service, hasn't every Sasanian government rewarded the Jews with land?"

"Joshwa!" his father said wearily.

"One king leaves, another takes his place. How many Jewish people did Behram hang? Zoroastrianism is the official religion of the Sasanian state. The crown has declared it." He went back to his book.

"The Aryans gave us shelter," Joshwa insisted.

"They only wanted us to unite with them in their war against the Romans," replied his father.

"And the Jews attacked and captured Isbahan," Joshwa shot back.

"And were shown no mercy," his father said coldly. "Hundreds of Jews were skinned alive."

"Why do you only want to remember the worst things, Abba?" Joshwa snapped.

"And what world are you living in?" his father retorted. He shut his book and turned to face Joshwa.

"Abba! Even the Christians live peacefully here under Aryan protection. They have never supported the Aryans in their war against the Romans, and never will."

"Indeed . . ." the old man sighed. "But that's different. Ever since the Romans embraced Christianity, the Aryans have grown to admire the Christians. A powerful empire is at their doorstep, one that shares their faith. The Aryans want to stay on favorable terms with the Christians."

He began to study the carpet spread across the floor, a vine of grapes running straight through its center, dividing it into two equal halves.

"Let's see what happens in Salukiyah . . . and what becomes of us after that."

Joshwa's mother entered the room. She wore a long, red cloak. A white scarf was wrapped around her head, concealing every strand of her salt-and-pepper hair.

"Come," she said softly, "dinner is ready."

The elderly man rose, leaning on his staff to steady himself, and slowly followed his wife and son out of the room. Age had tempered the once formidable presence of the patriarch. It had been a long time since he had given up the work of accounts altogether. Joshwa had taken his place. He was still unmarried—his only son!

"We're really worried about you, Joshwa."

"Worried?" Joshwa echoed as he sat down to eat at the *dastarkhwan*. "Nothing will happen to me . . . or to you. Abba, you're home all day. You don't know how much the Aryans respect your son—the laborers, the farmers, the craftsmen . . . Believe it or not, they wouldn't hesitate to lay down their lives for me."

As he spoke, Joshwa felt a flicker of embarrassment. *Am I being arrogant?*

"Indeed. I hear it all the time," said his father, a slight tremor in his voice.

"Don't they call you a filthy Jew?" asked Joshwa's mother, slicing a piece of grilled mutton from a large dish and offering it to her son.

Joshwa shook his head firmly. "Never!" he said, his mouth full.

* * *

Shapur Mehran crossed River Tigris and reached Salukiyah on the second day.

By then, his troops had encircled Salukiyah in a full siege. On the third morning, when the people of Salukiyah awoke, the Jews found their doors marked with bright red chalk. The King's army had completed the task overnight. A network of spies had been deployed in every major Sasanian city. Each spy operated under the guise of a merchant or tradesman. They recognized one another with a subtle signal—blinking their eyes.

At the break of dawn, these Jews were dragged out of their havelis, houses, and huts and herded into an open field. Before them was the commander-in-chief, astride a powerful horse. A hundred of the most respected among them were separated and led to a small courtyard nearby.

Shapur Mehran had spent the past two days pondering the fate of these people. He had concluded that physical torture was ultimately secondary, and that they could make do without it. The real objective was to strike fear in the prisoner's heart.

"Accursed Jews!" he thundered. "Wretched, ungrateful souls . . ." his eyes swept over the crowd. Among them, he recognized a few faces—landlords who had invited him over for dinners, accountants who kept the army's books in order, tax collectors without whom the machinery of the state could barely function—but he pressed on, his voice stern, his gaze unflinching.

"What comfort have you been denied in our kingdom? News of your mutiny reached the royal court without delay. Do not imagine for a moment that you can deceive us. Any threat to the Sasanian crown will be crushed swiftly."

The commander paused to stroke his horse's head, who was growing restless. Then, he turned to the crowd, their faces pale with fear. "Do you want to be cast out from this kingdom? To fall into the hands of the Romans? They are Christians. They will exact their revenge on each and every one of you for crucifying their apostle. Sweet, bloody revenge!" he cracked his whip sharply. The horse neighed loudly, pounding his hoofs on the ground, but Shapur pressed his thighs against its flanks to steady it.

"Three of your traitorous comrades who served in our Jewish company have been captured. They will be dragged across the mountains, their skin stretched tight, until all their flesh is stripped from their bodies, and the only thing left will be their veins clinging to the ropes."

He paused for a moment, then ordered:

"And as for you! From this moment on, you are forbidden to leave your palaces until the crown declares otherwise. Kneel!"

All the Jews in the red-brick courtyard fell to their knees. Turning his horse around, Shapur Mehran rode out of the courtyard and made his way to his tent. He felt confident that his threats had found their mark. Still, he ordered a few of his troops to stay behind in Salukiyah and guard the borders. He had also resolved to deploy the Jewish units of his army to a foreign province, one where the majority of the population was Christian and despised the Aryans. *Let them deal with the Armenians*, Shapur Mehran thought grimly. The Armenian region of the Sasanid empire was considered foreign territory, where every other day a new insurrection reared its head.

The next morning, the commander-in-chief of the Sasanian cavalry began his journey home. On his way, he stopped at a small Arya village on the eastern banks of the River Tigris—Baghdad. He had always been fond of their soft dates, which were used to make a delicious halwa. Carrying several bags filled with dates, he and his troops crossed the river.

CHAPTER 24

After Shapur Mehran's departure, the kneeling Jews raised their heads and brushed off the dust on their foreheads. Their elderly rabbi Mar-Zutra signaled them with his eyes to follow him inside his house. They were gathered in Mar-Zutra's haveli, the most beautiful Jewish building in Salukiyah.

"My children!" he spoke slowly and deliberately. "Our heads may bow under force, but our hearts must not . . . steel your hearts, children of Abraham."

The Jews seated on a large rug looked quietly at Mar-Zutra, their eyes filled with reverence. He was their Exilarch, a title first given by the Armenians to the rabbis of exiled Jews, now deeply woven into Jewish tradition. The Jews of Fars and Ctesiphon held Mar-Zutra in the highest esteem, whose young son Huna-Mari had been killed by the soldiers of King Peroz.

"Qobad has gotten a new idea in his head to turn the world upside down. He has fallen under Mazdak's spell, who insists that the wealth of the nobles be divided equally among all. Their men are adamant that Jews abandon their faith and convert. But we will safeguard our beliefs, my children."

"Noble saint," a young merchant spoke up. "Are they going back on their promise of religious freedom?"

Mar-Zutra was quiet for a while. Then, in a measured voice, he said: "Not yet. But that day is near when we will not be allowed to live by our own moral law."

The Jews sat deep in thought. Their elders had often told them that the Iranian kingdoms had not always been this way. Long ago, a few mobeds from an ordinary fire-temple in Istakhr had feigned an alliance with the Ashkanian kings, seizing control and ushering in the era of the Sasanian kings. It was these very kings who had declared Zoroastrianism to be the official religion of the Sasanian empire. And time and again, a Sasanian king—driven by religious zeal—would send his emissaries to the Jewish communities, insulting their dignity.

"Qobad has meddled before. Surely you remember the Mishnah affair?" said Mar-Zutra.

The Mishnah affair had become infamous among the Jews. Mishnah, a boy from their community, had fallen in love with a Zoroastrian girl. He couldn't marry her, but carnal relations had developed between them, something his neighbors could confirm. According to Jewish law, the wretched girl had to be put to death. But here, on this foreign land governed by Zoroastrians, they were powerless to harm her. They could, however, punish a Jew in recompense. On Mar-Zutra's order, Mishnah was publicly flogged with twenty lashes, but that traitor Mishnah had lodged a complaint with the ruler of Salukiyah, and Qobad's men had arrived to look into the matter. For months, they had hounded prominent members of the Jewish community, disrupting their lives.

"We do not interfere in your methods of taxation, which you are free to align with Jewish law. But when it comes to taking a life or administering torture, the crown will always have a say, especially in matters decided without the knowledge of our scribes and scholars," they insisted.

The Jews had placated the Sasanian emissaries by bribing them with bars of pure gold. But within a few short years, the occasional cries of "religious freedom for all" gave way to the slogan "one kingdom, one religion." Some Sasanian kings considered Zoroastrianism as a means to unify the kingdom, and it became clear that their true aim was to see every subject become Zoroastrian.

"These misguided souls will never succeed in erasing a people chosen by Elohim himself to bring order to the world," Mar-Zutra said with conviction.

The audience shifted restlessly on the rug. Not one of them believed anymore that they had been chosen to bring order to the world, nor did they care. All that was left was fatigue—a despair that had been their fate for generations. If they converted to Zoroastrianism, they would lose the few privileges and rights they had as Jews. But the Zoroastrian farmer, craftsman, and slave lived in far harsher conditions than them. And then what was the final destiny of religious converts but to be lost among a faceless crowd? Even at that very moment, when hundreds of the poor were converting to Mazdakism each day and flocking to Ctesiphon, thousands of Jews wrestled with the question of how to preserve their identity. Heaven only knew when they would reach the promised land. But for now, they needed a free, sovereign state of their own. No matter how small.

"Are you with me, my children?" Mar-Zutra asked.

The room shook with the chorus of voices.

"We are—we are all with you, our lord Exilarch."

"We must make our way to Mohaza. We depart tonight," said Mar-Zutra.

Mohaza was a big Jewish settlement in Ctesiphon. Unlike Salukiyah, it had no population of Nasrani people, whose coexistence with the Jews had been impossible.

The crowd left the Exilarch's haveli with earnest resolve. *You only know how to wield your might against the unarmed, Aryans,* their minds raced. *Come and face the Jewish youth!*

In the coming months, Mohaza and its neighboring regions were on the verge of declaring Jewish freedom and sovereignty within the Sasanian state. The Jewish units of the Sasanian cavalry were coming in droves to join the cause, and the borders of Mohaza had transformed into an impenetrable stronghold. Shapur Mehran's troops found themselves in constant combat with the defending forces. The people of Mohaza erected a defensive wall around the city in no time, and their shovels dug a deep trench around it. The trench was so wide that not even the most powerful Sasanian steeds could leap across.

"Those who rise against us will find themselves hell-bound!" Mar-Zutra's voice rang in the city square.

"Hell-bound!" the young men echoed in unison, raising their shovels in defiance. Hell—a place of raging fire, where according to Jewish belief, the wicked would burn until they were mere cinders. *And yet, the Zoroastrians worship this malevolent, foul substance!* they marveled. *Thousands, hundreds of thousands! Verily*, they thought, *this is the fate of whomever Elohim chooses to forsake!*

Jewish leaders were dreaming of defeating the Sasanians and building a small Jewish kingdom like the Sasanian court. Unlike the Sasanians, their king would not take "many wives," as that was forbidden in the Torah. No. Just an appropriate number.

Their nobles and merchants were content with two, three, or at most four wives. As Mar-Zutra often clarified: "Not more than two to four . . . so that you may visit each after a period of time. And as the Torah and Talmud command, give each her own home. Do not keep them under the same roof . . . reason itself demands the same."

"Our religion aligns with nature," the Exilarch preached. "The Nasranis have invented their own ways. But human needs—and the Jews—do not change. Not long ago, when the Christians had not yet started this Nestorian business, Roman emperor Herod took a second wife while the first still lived. It was only through Jewish law that his marriage was deemed lawful," he reminded his devoted listeners.

CHAPTER 25

"It's the law of air," Mazdak explained to Jawani, placing a hand on his throat.

He had come to the Sufi shrine after many days. Preoccupied with life, he hadn't found the time to share the quiet stirrings in the depths of his heart with anyone. Most of his day was spent with Joshwa once his friend returned from school.

Jawani was from Arabistan. He wasn't a Bedouin, but the son of an *attar* merchant from Hirah. He had arrived in Ctesiphon on a camel laden with fragrant woods, stones, and herbs. He spent the night in a caravanserai. When he awoke the next morning, he found that all his goods had been stolen during the night.

"Has anyone seen my camel?" he asked passersby as he desperately wandered the streets of Ctesiphon. The cunning people of the capital city paid him no mind. Jawani felt utterly disillusioned in the world. How could he go back home now? His father already thought he was good for nothing. And so, Jawani had no choice but to seek refuge in the Sufi shrine. As he watered the plants, he was startled to find a peace he had never known before, not even when he sold all his goods, nor when he returned home with bags full of dinars and dirhams. Here, they gave him a simple porridge made of wheat and barley twice a day. And today . . . today the new prophet of the Zoroastrians had come. Jawani sat before him, hands folded in respect.

"Do you hear me?" asked Mazdak, then started to laugh. "Of course! You must hear me—I speak, and you listen!"

Jawani had started to grasp their language. He nodded. Mazdak went on:

"This . . ." he pressed his hand against his throat once more: "This is a place of possibility. Infinite, endless possibility. The tremor of the whole universe—of time, of space, of circumstance—it resonates here. This . . . this is where the world was born. The voice. Words—words that issue from the mouth and make us you and I."

"The wonders of Uzza!" Jawani burst out.

At his reaction, another Irfani standing nearby laughed heartily: "You are remembering Uzza? Indeed! Why not? We will make a statuette in honor of Uzza. Let's send for the sculptor."

Jawani gave the Irfani a look of gratitude. Shame was an emotion left behind, far outside the four walls of this sanctuary. Nobody shamed him here over anything. But the new prophet of the Zoroastrians was not Irfani. Rather than accept the world, he had made up his mind to change it.

"Justice is the urge of the human soul," said Mazdak.

"But," the Irfani said uncertainly, "with your permission, the farmers and craftsmen have seized the wealth of the nobles. Why was it seized?"

"Because they weren't giving it freely," Mazdak smiled. "So we were forced to seize it."

Then, he added:

"The looting in Ctesiphon has ceased, my dear Irfani. Joshwa has balanced the books and the King has made laws."

"But we are getting news of riots from other cities," said the Irfani.

"The King will put an end to them," Mazdak reassured him.

"How can you be so sure? Once the riots are set in motion, who will stop them?"

"Shapur Mehran," Mazdak said with another smile.

The Irfani smiled back. He had thought Mazdak's answer would be Ahura Mazda.

"Long live Shapur Mehran!" the Irfani chanted.

Mazdak departed, his steps measured. He was to meet Shapur Mehran in the evening. After Joshwa, the kind, well-intentioned commander-in-chief was his greatest ally.

CHAPTER 26

Lead the cavalry without bloodshed . . . is that even possible? Lying on his comfortable bed, the commander-in-chief Shapur Mehran wondered. It was at the behest of his beloved prophet that King Qobad had given this command. His enemies scoffed at him, the nobles and scribes laughing behind his back. *What kind of a king is afraid of spilling blood? Coward!* They sneered. *This is the end of the Sasanian empire. A sly shepherd could seize his crown with just two strikes of his stick!*

"It isn't right!" Shapur Mehran thought, tossing in bed. "At least not while I'm alive." But the times were perilous. To crush the Jewish uprising, his troops were locked in combat on all four borders of Mohaza. The Jews were fighting valiantly. Their poison-tipped arrows sliced clean through Sasanian armor. *My cavalry needs reinforcements*, reflected the commander. His troops had not been trained to fight Bedouins. They were an organized force, primed to confront Roman legions—not the Bedouins, who would leap like a band of langurs and vanish into thin air, only to reemerge from behind a thicket of cypress trees. *Perhaps it's time to call on the Hunan tribes. If anyone can contend with the Bedouins, it's them.*

Shapur Mehran lowered the glow of his lamp. Shadows moved on the carpeted floor. The commander dismissed them at first, then studied the shapes closely.

It was two of them. Two shadows. Shapur turned abruptly.

"Who is it? Who's there?"

His voice died in his throat as a shadow climbed onto his chest and pinned him down. Another figure shoved a wad of cloth into his mouth. The glint of a dagger as it moved toward his neck. Shapur Mehran thrashed, his eyeballs darting in their sockets like wounded pigeons. He tried to buck them off with one swift motion, but the blade was quicker. It plunged into his neck, slicing clean through his gullet to the pillow beneath. A gurgling sound escaped his throat. His head jerked sharply to the right, then stilled. The sound was muffled by the wad of cloth.

"Filthy traitor . . ." a hiss filled the room. "Had we the time, we would make you suffer nine deaths."

There was a faint rustling sound, and then a gaping silence filled the room.

CHAPTER 27

Five days' journey from Ctesiphon at a short distance from the city of Zardoq, a sudden bend in the path gave way to the towering flintstone fortress, visible from miles away. This was the Fortress of the Forgotten Ones, a place whose very mention was forbidden in the Sasanid kingdom.

A small caravan advanced toward the fortress—twenty-five horsemen escorting King Qobad. They had left Ctesiphon under the cover of night, camped out in tents the next day, and resumed their journey through the night. These were handpicked men, the most loyal among Sufra's faithful ranks. Their faces were concealed behind masks of thick black cloth. They did not even know each other's names.

Qobad, king of the Sasanian empire until just a day ago, had been dethroned by an alliance of nobles and intellectuals. Now, he was bound for the fortress, destined to spend his remaining days in exile. Throughout the kingdom, even speaking his name had been strictly prohibited.

On the journey, they appointed one among them to ride to the city whenever they needed fresh vegetables, fruits, paan, and meat. Supplies from Zardoq took longer than usual. The food bearer returned late. That day, the guards were so busy cooking they failed to notice that the horseman they had sent was lying tied up under a tree. Riding his horse, wearing his clothes and mask was someone else . . . It was Seyavash, who had been trailing the caravan for three days in pursuit of the palanquin carrying his beloved king. He had sworn to remain faithful to the King until his dying breath. Now was the time to fulfill that vow.

Qobad sat with his back against a boulder near the palanquin, his eyes locked on the horizon. Goshtasp and his allies had not wasted a day getting to Ctesiphon. Taking full advantage of the unrest that ensued after the murder of commander-in-chief Shapur Mehran, they stormed the royal palace with their private armies and took the King hostage in his own bed chamber. From behind a gold-embroidered curtain, Jamasp trembled as he watched the scene unfold. He wanted to flee the palace, but Goshtasp's men had recognized him.

"Where are you going, Your Majesty?" Goshtasp asked him respectfully.

Your Majesty? Jamasp wondered. *Am I to be crowned king?* Fourteen-year-old Jamasp was befuddled.

"And Qobad? What do we do with him?" he asked. Goshtasp had proposed that Qobad be executed immediately.

"But my lord . . . he is not unpopular. His execution could lead to chaos," the nobles expressed their fears.

Then, the newly elected mobed had presented his scheme: "Qobad must be imprisoned in the Fortress of the Forgotten Ones. He will stay there for the remainder of his life. To utter his name will be forbidden. Over time, he will be erased from memory."

After some hesitation, the nobles had agreed to this solution.

And now, Goshtasp's men were leading him to his final destination.

Final destination! thought Qobad. He could feel the blood coursing through his veins. He was healthy and active. Despite these tragic times, he was eating heartily to keep his strength up. He was determined that he would not be locked up in the fortress for long. He would escape, and raise a new army. He would take his kingdom back . . . but how? The plan hadn't yet revealed itself to him.

A guard put a tray of food before him, and gently squeezed his hand. Alarmed, Qobad stared at the guard. A pair of bright, smiling brown eyes looked back at him from behind the mask. How could he forget those eyes? Qobad's own eyes lit up, as if kindled by the light in his friend's eyes.

"Seyavash!"

The cherished name reached his lips, only to retreat in silence. Seyavash quickly nodded and turned back. He watched the other guards to make sure no one had witnessed him signal the King.

Qobad felt relieved and light. Seyavash was here with him. Soon, Naindokht would also learn his whereabouts. But where was Naindokht herself? The Sasanian queen and Prince Khosrow were nowhere to be found in the palace. Goshtasp's soldiers failed to find her even on the day of Jamasp's crowning, two days after Goshtasp stormed the palace with his army. His men had turned Ctesiphon upside down looking for the queen and her son, but because of the unexpected unrest that had spread in the city, they hadn't been able to find them.

* * *

The Fortress of the Forgotten Ones.

Through a tall, wide archway stood the great hall, its walls shimmering with intricate gold-and-silver inlay. The doors of several spacious, interconnected rooms opened into the grand hall. Beyond it lay a chamber that had likely once housed the King's privy council. Beside it was a sprawling garden, its lofty trees long since cut down to prevent anyone from hiding behind them. But the garden was abundant in flowering plants and delicate, trailing vines. Lush green grass blanketed the ground. At the far end of the garden were the kitchen and servant quarters. The bedrooms were furnished with comfortable seating and beds. Cushioned chairs lined the rooms, and niches in the walls held stacks of decorative cups and plates. A prison built for important royal captives, it was furnished with every comfort. The fortress had been designed with one principle in mind: that its prisoners feel comfortable, and that the thought of escaping rarely cross their minds. A few miles from here on top of a small hill was the prisoner's final resting place. The corpse was laid out on the *dokhma* for birds of prey, who fed on its flesh until it became one with their own blood and bone. Perched on the hill and in the trees around it, flocks of vultures waited patiently for the next arrival. Meanwhile, they visited nearby villages, where food was never scarce and their stomachs could be filled with ease.

Who came here, and when they arrived—not even Qobad remembered. To speak the names of those imprisoned in the fortress had always been strictly forbidden. This tactic proved so effective that their names had faded entirely from the memory of the people.

CHAPTER 28

Wrapped in a big black shawl, her face hidden, Naindokht stepped inside Mazdak's haveli. She had arrived on a small carriage drawn to a donkey. She was accompanied by her son Khosrow, whom she had left outside in the carriage. The usher did not recognize her.

"And you are?" he asked.

"Tell Bamdad *babajan* that his aunt is here to see him," replied Naindokht.

The usher had just been roused from a deep sleep. Rubbing his eyes, he knocked on Bamdad's door. When Bamdad opened his door, Naindokht uncovered her face. For a moment, Bamdad forgot to breathe.

"Your Majesty, my queen!" he whispered.

"Babajan!" Naindokht exclaimed. "I am here to see the Prophet's wife."

Bamdad did not ask questions. These were unusual times. King Qobad had been exiled, and the queen had come to his house draped in a tattered black shawl.

"Denag . . . my niece," said Bamdad. "She is not here. She is . . . outside . . . in the quarter," Bamdad spoke haltingly. "She is impure these days."

Impure! Naindokht's thoughts raced. A plan was taking shape in her mind.

The usher escorted Naindokht to a room outside the haveli. He pounded his staff on the ground to wake the lady of the house.

Denag was sleeping on the bare floor. Until she performed the ritual bath of purification, she was not permitted to sleep on the bed. Naindokht helped Denag get up. The women sat down on two comfortable chairs lined up against the wall.

"I do not have much time, Denag," said Naindokht. Try as she might, she spoke in the unmistakable tone of a queen. Though in that moment, her thoughts were only of Qobad.

"At your word, Your Highness," said Denag, her eyes widening.

Placing the oil lamp on an alcove in the wall, the usher left the room. Naindokht started talking:

"My faithful friend, I have found out where the King is being held. I must attempt to rescue him. But to leave the city, I need to disguise myself." Then, she looked closely at Denag: "Where is the Prophet, Denag?

Denag's face clouded over.

"I do not know, my queen," she answered. Then, she turned to the queen attentively: "I am at your command, Your Majesty. How can I help?"

"Go into hiding for a few days. Lend me your carriage and garments. I shall flee Ctesiphon in your guise. I must go to Khuzestan, where the fortress is located. By putting my life on the line, I may yet free the King."

Denag dragged herself across the room to a chest. She extracted her clothes, wrapped them in a bundle, and gave it to Naindokht. The queen left one of her own attires on Denag's bed.

"My carriage will be at your door tomorrow morning. Or would you like to spend the night here?"

"No," said Naindokht. "The prince will be here for the carriage tomorrow morning." She bent down and planted a kiss on Denag's cheek. "I am very sorry about your illness," she added politely. The kind-hearted queen was saddened by Denag's disability.

That is the reason Mazdak does not love his king-wife, said a small voice in her head.

Naindokht walked toward the door. Suddenly, she stopped and turned.

"Denag, if you can menstruate, you can become a mother, too. Why did the Prophet . . ." her voice trailed off. *Why did he not try?*

Denag watched wide-eyed in the dark as the queen departed.

A short distance away from the haveli, Khosrow waited in the carriage for his mother. His hands were coated with dust, as if he were a common laborer, and a black cloth was wrapped around his head, concealing his face.

"You are late, honored mother."

"My dear son . . . I had to tell them everything," Naindokht looked at her son with warmth. "The noble prophet was not home."

"Noble prophet!" Khosrow said with contempt. "Had he been here, I would have ended his life today, right now. Is he not the cause of our family's misfortunes? Is he not the one who misled the King?"

The queen rebuked her son in the wobbling carriage.

"No, Khosrow . . . your tender-hearted father felt the pain of his people. The nobles and priests had already resolved to dethrone the King a long time ago . . . long before he met Mazdak."

Khosrow did not respond to his mother. They had arranged to depart at dawn. In Khuzestan, a gulf along the Karun River served as a mooring place for merchant ships from Hind. It was possible they might slip aboard one of these vessels with Qobad and set sail for the Indian subcontinent. That was Naindokht's wish—to take her husband and precious son far, far away from a land that had turned against them overnight.

CHAPTER 29

"Your hands and feet are mighty fair! Show us your face, will you?" one of the guards posted at the entrance to the fortress said to a tall woman wrapped in a raggedy black shawl. She carried a heavy pot in each hand. She had come from a nearby village to collect scraps and trash. Often, the people in her village found useful things among the fortress's discarded waste. It wasn't unusual for a village woman like her to turn up at the fortress every so often.

"May your words choke you!" the woman shot back in her fluent village dialect. "Move it—out of my way!"

In haste, she passed under the archway and stepped into the great hall. On either side stood gold-plated doors, all locked and bolted. Naindokht's heart was pounding. She could hear it loud and clear.

"One . . . two . . . three . . . four . . ." she counted each door she passed, trying to calm her nerves. The fifth door was not locked. Naindokht gave it a gentle push, and it swung open without a sound. Naindokht slipped inside and closed the door behind her.

"My king! Light of my eyes!" she spoke softly. Qobad stood next to a window, gazing out at the endless stretch of barren land. He started. Naindokht took off her shawl and moved toward him, arms wide. Overcome with joy, Qobad rushed to her, and they fell into each other's arms. Naindokht's tears soaked through his cloak.

"I have come to rescue you," she said at last.

"Rescue me . . . but how?"

They were sitting on the bed, speaking in hushed voices.

"You wait and see, my king," said Naindokht.

"And Khosrow? Where is he?"

"He awaits us in a nearby village. Do not worry. He's in disguise. Shall we leave for Hind, Your Highness?" Naindokht asked, her eyes brimming with love.

"What are you saying!" Qobad said firmly. "I will go to the Hephthalites. They are my allies. We will take our kingdom back from those traitors."

"But Seyavash . . ." Naindokht began, hesitant.

"Seyavash has arranged everything with me," Qobad told her. "My beloved, loyal friend . . . he'll join us along the way with his troops."

Seyavash had hidden Naindokht in a vizier's empty haveli. After that one time, Seyavash had not been able to visit her again, so Naindokht had made the rest of the plan on her own.

"We only have a few moments to spend together," Naindokht reminded Qobad.

They lay back in bed, wrapped tightly in each other's arms.

On her way back, the village woman carried a heavy bundle of supplies, wrapped up in a large floor rug she dragged behind her.

The guards at the gate instantly closed in on her.

"What are you making off with? We need to inspect you."

"Kind sirs," the woman said in her village twang. "I just want to say that I'm impure this week. These are my dirty, blood-stained clothes that I'll be washing at home."

As soon as they heard the word "impure," the guards jumped back as if stung by scorpions. Now they didn't want to touch her or her bundle with a ten-foot pole. From the edge of the bundle, a few of the woman's garments peeked out, blackened with bloodstains. Naindokht had brought Denag's contaminated clothes with her. She herself was perfectly pure.

"Out, out you go!" the guard snapped.

Dragging her bundle behind her, Naindokht disappeared into the distance. But the guards remained fearful. They had seen polluted garments. When they returned home in six months, after their shifts changed, they would pay penance to their mobeds to atone for their sin.

CHAPTER 30

Qobad arrived in the khanate of the White Huns in full splendor. Led by Seyavash, ten thousand troops marched in the King's retinue. Their flags rippled in the strong winds, the famed leather print of the Derafsh Kaviani—the legendary Sasanian standard—emblazoned upon them: a crimson square, four yellow petals set against a violet field, and at the center, a small flower like a sunburst. This was the blacksmith's banner, the one who had defeated Zahhak, and whose story had been passed down generations of Aryans.

Galloping like the wind to welcome them were the tall, handsome horsemen of Hunan. Their flags streamed in the wind, the god riding a bull woven into their cloth seeming to charge alongside the horsemen.

Past the welcoming soldiers, Hephthalite tents stretched endlessly into the distance. The Great Khan, leader of the Hephthalites, was waiting for them in a sprawling silk tent. The Hephthalite army swept Qobad's troops into the heart of the camp. Qobad, Naindokht, and Khosrow were presented to the Khan inside his tent.

The moment their eyes met, a flood of memories surged through both Qobad and the Khan. This was not Qobad's first time before the emperor. When he was just seven or eight years old, the emperor had taken Qobad to the khanate as a hostage. At the time, it was not unusual for Hephthalites to attack the Sasanians. Qobad's father, King Peroz, had declared war on the Hephthalites, and lost. When the Hun emperor demanded ransom, it was discovered that the Sasanian treasury was all but empty. And so, the Khan took what was most precious to Peroz: his son. Qobad has spent three years of his youth in the Khan and his wife's tents. He had gone horseback riding on the lightning-fast, regal horses of the Hephthalite men, and the wife of the Great Khan had often fed him with her own hands. During those years, they had developed an intimate bond with each other. After three years, Peroz was finally able to pay the ransom in full, and the emperor was compelled to send Qobad back. His eyes had welled up with tears. The Khan and his wife did not have any children back then.

The Khan has aged, thought Qobad. He remembered the young emperor, who used to come charging on his horse at such a great speed brandishing his spear that foam would fly out of the horse's mouth.

Gone is that small, skinny boy . . . what a fine young man Qobad has become! the Khan thought affectionately. He smiled.

"Come here, sit with me," he said.

Qobad bowed and touched the Khan's feet in obeisance. For a moment, he forgot that he was the leader of the Sasanian empire. King of Kings, whom the courtiers called lord of the two worlds. All he remembered was the fatherly affection that the Great Khan had showered over a child who was entirely at his mercy.

The emperor embraced Qobad, who respectfully took a seat by his side.

"I have heard the Sasanid mobeds and nobles have gravely wronged you. They always were fools," the Khan said in the Hephthalite language.

Something stirred in Qobad's memory. The long forgotten Hephthalite language suddenly seemed to come alive on his tongue. Haltingly, he began to speak:

"Yes, Your Highness. But I have every intention of reclaiming my throne," said Qobad.

The Khan's servants laid out a *dastarkhwan* upon the priceless carpets. The moment the linen covers were lifted from the platters of food, plumes of aromatic steam wafted up and filled the tent.

"I wish to give the princess's hand to you in marriage," the emperor said tenderly as he ate.

"The princess!" Qobad repeated, surprised. Then, it came to him in a flash. The Khan had wanted to convert war into friendship. He had expressed a desire to marry Peroz's daughter. But Peroz could not bear that his daughter, raised in the comfort and luxury of the Sasanian palace, leave her indulgent life behind to live among nomads. He had sent his most beautiful handmaid in his daughter's stead, laden with magnificent tributes, along with a message claiming that the maid was his daughter. The handmaid was strikingly beautiful, with pleasing manners, so the Khan had not suspected a thing. Later, rumors of Peroz's deception reached the khanate, but by then, the Khan had grown close to his lovely wife, who was now the mother of their newborn daughter, and the emperor's only child. The Hephthalite father—initially known as "Hephthali" among the Sasanians, then eventually as "Abdali"—and the mother of Fars had birthed a seed that had bloomed into a remarkable beauty, her skin like milk touched with rose, her figure finely sculpted.

“Is Her Majesty the princess unmarried still? Qobad asked with obvious curiosity.

“No, no!” the Khan smiled. “One of our commanders is her husband. But rest assured, she will give you preference.”

“Ah!” said Qobad. He recalled that Abdali women took multiple husbands, just like the Sasanian men took multiple wives.

To each their own, he marveled.

“It would be my honor, Your Highness. I would consider myself most fortunate to be blessed with the title of your son-in-law,” Qobad said humbly.

That night in his tent, when Qobad relayed the whole story to Naindokht, her heart sank. Since the day he married her, he had never even looked at another woman. He had even decided to give the angelic beauty from Hirah to one of his sons. Overcome with grief and fury, Naindokht began to cry. She resolved that she would poison the Khan’s daughter.

“Come now, don’t weep, my darling,” Qobad reassured her. “I need an alliance with the Abdalis. These fearless fighters and foot soldiers can help me get my kingdom back. You know your place is in my heart. And in any case, the Hun Princess Sera would spend most of her time with her first husband.”

“What?” Naindokht looked at him with alarm.

“Abdali women have many husbands,” Qobad explained.

Naindokht listened to Qobad in awe. “Is that really true?”

How colorful was the world, and how little she knew about it. Qobad was telling her that the women could take several husbands—first at their fathers’ command, and later by their husbands’ choice. When it comes to offspring, though, only the children from the first husband are considered rightful.

Children! All of a sudden, Naindokht thought of Khosrow, who was sound asleep in his room.

"You must not bed this Hephthalite woman," she said tearfully.

"Alright. I promise."

But Naindokht's heart was unmoved. She knew that Qobad could not go through with his promise. At that moment, Khosrow was all she could think about. Her son was the culmination of her life's work. She wanted to take him to a sanctuary far away from this cursed khanate. Her son! Her Khosrow!

"Why do these women remarry so many times, simply at the command of their father or husband?"

"Why?" Qobad echoed. "What power do poor women really have?"

Naindokht had been sobbing quietly, and was about to drift off. Suddenly, as if in a dream, she was struck with a thought that jolted her awake. She turned to Qobad, and said:

"What power do women have? I am the one who rescued you from imprisonment. Me!"

Qobad was taken aback. After a few moments, he said: "That is because you are my darling. Now go to sleep, my king-wife. That is you, and only you."

Qobad was satisfied with his answer. It was his habit to dismiss women as insignificant, useful only when he needed them to do his bidding. No one ever stopped to question the contradiction between those two extremes. By Prophet Mazdak's decree, women were to be equally distributed among men. Even the poorest farmer had a right to a wife, but keeping more than one was no longer permitted. But Qobad was remarrying simply out of necessity. Surely Prophet Mazdak would understand his predicament. Given that in the eyes of the one true religion, it would be a sin, but one could pay penance to the mobeds for sinning. Such was the custom under the old faith, and what a wise ritual it had been! Qobad mourned its passing. *It must be reinstated—this time under the banner of the one true faith!* He knew, as did everyone else, that a man would do as he pleased, or as necessity compelled him. And if it was a sin, well, that's what penance was for. What a blessing it was! Setting people free from the guilt of sin.

Feeling reassured, Qobad fell asleep. A small part of him was looking forward to the new wedding.

The next morning, Naindokht bade Khosrow farewell as she entrusted him to Seyavash.

"Your king is soon to marry the Khan's daughter. Take your crown prince to a safe place. His life is in danger here." Then, she added: "Seyavash! Find out where Prophet Mazdak is, and how he is."

Seyavash was reminded of his friend. Having successfully rescued the Sasanian crown from the enemy's lair, he suddenly missed his home, his land, and his friend. *Where are you, Mazdak?* he wondered anxiously.

* * *

Mazdak was in Ctesiphon.

The highways and streets of Ctesiphon were in pandemonium. A throng of farmers arriving from the villages, including craftsmen from the city, flocked toward the Prophet's haveli. Jamasp's men failed to contain them. The crowd had taken Mazdak's haveli into their protective custody.

"Let it be known . . ." said the chief mobed, stroking his beard, "that we give our word Mazdak will not be harmed. Perhaps then we might be rid of these wretched farmers, and they will return to work in the fields."

"That is very important," a wealthy merchant piped up. "Otherwise what will we eat, lord?"

The decree had been brought before Jamasp as a mere formality. He readily signed on the fine vellum. Everything that was going on in Ctesiphon was beyond the young king's comprehension. Whenever he held court, he pardoned every criminal. The nobles tried to advise him, but their counsel was wasted on the naïve king. Goshtasp had already moved the major portion of the royal treasury to his havelis. But the cavalry had to be paid their monthly dues, so Goshtasp had to force the nobles to provide the money for the troops. This angered the nobles. Seyavash's troops, the bravest and most skilled soldiers in the Sasanian cavalry who were unparalleled in the art of warcraft, had disappeared from the cavalry. The remaining troops were engaged with the Jewish traitors on the borders of Mohaza.

As if this weren't enough of a headache for the nobles, the ruler of Armenia—an important part of the Sasanian empire—announced that he wanted a free and sovereign state. In haste, one regiment headed to Armenia.

"Lord King! What should we do with those traitors?"

"Pardon them," Jamasp replied lightly.

"Your Majesty, the farmers and craftsmen are looting the havelis of the nobles."

"Is that so?" asked the King. He seemed genuinely surprised. "Are they still doing all that?"

A dejected and regretful Goshtasp stood before the King. If there were a way to acquire royal lineage, he would have easily run the kingdom on his own. But that was impossible. *After all,* he thought, *murdering a commander-in-chief in the cover of night and governing the Sasanian empire are not one and the same.* If the peasants obeyed anyone's orders, he could be finished off. But they were protecting Mazdak. Day or night, it made no difference to them. All night, they lit small fires and gathered around them, singing folk songs.

Qobad! Goshtasp thought.

Could it be that after the great struggle to dethrone Qobad and banish him to the Fortress of the Forgotten Ones, Goshtasp missed him? Qobad had spent only a few days there before escaping, fleeing to the Hunan Khanate for refuge. Would he return with the White Huns to attack them?

Goshtasp brooded in silence.

CHAPTER 31

When her maidservants helped Denag to her bedroom after her purification bath, she eyed the dress that Naindokht had left for her in her polluted room.

A shimmering cloak of pure white silk brocade, its neckline and sleeves richly embroidered with threads of gold and silver. The cloak was adorned with true white pearls. The ensemble came with a delicate white turban, crowned by the brilliant plumage of a yellow bird.

"Help me into this dress," she commanded. She looked at her reflection in the wrought-iron mirror. The stark white of the turban set off her mane of dark curls. Her maidservants dabbed her cheeks lightly with rouge, and plucked her eyebrows. They finished by perfuming her with a mist that breathed of springtime blossoms.

That night when Mazdak came home, he carried a round tray of food to his wife's room, as was his habit. As he approached the door, he froze. Putting the tray down on a stool, he rubbed his eyes. What he saw was impossible. Lying asleep on Denag's bed with her face toward the wall was Naindokht.

Naindokht!

The Sasanian queen—she who was Ahura Mazda's creation and his will. Denag turned on her side. "Ah!" Mazdak drew in his breath. It was Denag. But . . . was this really Denag? She was breathtaking! His heart surged with wonder and disappointment. He extended his arm to help Denag up in bed, and touched Naindokht's garments.

Naindokht took his hand. She pulled Mazdak into her arms.

Mazdak sank into the soft, gold-embroidered folds of the queen's silken gown. A heavenly fragrance wrapped around them. It felt like standing on the deck of a great ship, hands clutching the rail, rising with the crest of a towering wave—higher, still higher—as the clear blue sky drew nearer . . . and nearer . . .

Rain began to fall, drumming against the roof of the haveli. It was raining in Ctesiphon. Rain, at last! Lightning flashed, illuminating the room. Thunder cracked open the clouds. Denag wrapped the Prophet in her arms. *This union will bring forth a beautiful child,* she thought. *He will not be a prophet. He will be mine—he will stay with me.*

Outside the haveli, the peasants—who just a few moments ago had been half-asleep, half-awake—were now fully alert, shouting with joy. They sang and danced in the rain as they celebrated the long-awaited downpour. The water had extinguished all the fires save one, which the farmers had refused to let die. They had built a ring of stones around it, guarding its flame.

Lightning split the sky open, dividing the heavens in two. Crimson streaks tore through the blackness. Deafening bursts of thunder roared overhead, and the skies burst open again. Rain poured down once more. Barzin stood beneath a tree with Shu Wan, his Chinese friend and silk weaver. The sensation of raindrops against his skin inspired the weaver's imagination with carnal fantasies. Enraptured, Shu Wan leaned in and spoke in Barzin's ear:

"We begin with three, then two . . . then six times at once . . . then, we enter . . ."

Shu Wan found himself fantasizing about the newly arrived nobleman's bride—delicate and beautiful—in the haveli across the River Tigris. Perhaps this time he might succeed in capturing her.

Barzin turned to him with amused surprise: "My friend . . . how are you able to count at a time like this!"

"It's a force of habit," said the Khotani youth with a wise nod. His eyes were slanted, his skin the color of ivory.

Barzin considered this for a moment. Then, he slapped his thigh and burst out laughing—a sound that echoed across the sky. His laughter mingled with the sounds of rain. Barzin laughed all night at this notion. *No doubt*, he thought, *my friend is a lover of numbers*. Even while weaving silk, he would trace invisible numbers on the floor with a thin wooden stick.

Inside the haveli, sprawled on his back on Denag's bed, Bamdad's son smiled in the darkness. His one arm cradled his head, while the other was wrapped around Denag. He gently stroked her arm. From the window, he watched the pouring sky outside.

"First, Ahura Mazda created the sky. Then, he made water, and water lives in all of us. It is the sap in trees, and the rain pouring down from the skies infuses trees with its moisture. Within that moisture is warmth. And fire—the sacred fire—is its companion."

Mazdak recited the Avesta under his breath. Why had he deprived himself of happiness all these years? All his life, he advised others to extract joy out of life, and yet he forgot to remind himself of the same thing?! But regret served no purpose now. He was alive, and from this moment on, he would spend every night by Denag's side.

"And then, Ahura Mazda created the earth. Then, he made lush, green plants . . . then animals . . . and then, humans . . . and everything he created was for all humanity alike."

The Prophet recited the verse and blew on Denag's face. Instinctively, Denag closed her eyes, and laughed.

CHAPTER 32

The Roman emperor Flavius Petrus Sabbatius Justinian was feeling dejected and anxious. He had not yet found the time to meet with his Sasanian guests—an army commander and a young prince. The commander had introduced himself as Seyavash; the prince was the son of the dethroned King Qobad. Seyavash had brought a proposal: that Justinian adopt the prince, Khosrow, as his own and allow him to stay with him. Such a request was neither new nor unheard of at that time. The Sasanian king Yazdegerd I had once adopted Theodosius, son of the Roman emperor Caesar Arcadius, and became his mentor. When it came to protecting their sons in the midst of war, who better to turn to but one another? Between these ancient empires, such gestures had long smoothed the princes' path to the throne.

Now that the Sasanian kingdom lay in the hands of a young and naïve king, it was an opportune moment for the Romans to attack. Perhaps for that very reason, the deposed king had entrusted his son to them. Though Qobad was stripped of his crown, his son remained the rightful heir to the Sasanian throne by blood, and may still become king. Justinian found himself facing a grave dilemma. He could not consult his commander-in-chief, as he was leading the Roman legion to Hispania, where the empire sought once more to reassert its dominion. For decades, the region had been under the rule of the Goths. It was imperative to reclaim it. But what consumed Justinian was the unrest that was spreading like wildfire within Christendom. A serious disagreement about the nature of Jesus Christ, that had started off as theological speculation but had grown into open dissent. To maintain solidarity in the kingdom, it was critical to put an end to the discord.

Caesar Justinian summoned the Sasanian guests to appear before the court. However, at that very moment, he was engaged in dialogue with Syrian clerics and other religious leaders from the capital city. A message was dispatched to Seyavash, instructing him to wait until the conclusion of the discussion.

Accompanied by the young prince, Seyavash settled into a comfortable seat in the imperial court. An elderly priest—his face radiant and framed by a flowing beard—had arrived from Syria. He spoke in Greek:

"Lord King, the Father, the Son, and the Holy Spirit cannot be three separate persons. Surely they co-existed in the person of Jesus upon the cross." He paused. "Christ himself was God."

"Was he not human, then?" the delegate of the cabinet from Constantinople asked mockingly.

"He was both human and God. The two aspects were united in a single person," said the Syrian delegate. "If they were separate persons, then the Father would have precedence over the Son. And how could anyone have precedence over Jesus Christ? He *was* God."

"But Your Majesty," the delegate from Constantinople now addressed the Caesar directly: "The apostles of Christ, Matthew in particular, have written plainly in the New Testament. Jesus said: *I speak only what was spoken to me by my Father*. Consider this,

Your Highness—the Father was not the Savior, and the Savior was not the Holy Spirit. These are three distinct aspects. The complete Godhead is found in the trinity."

The Syrian theologian struck his staff against the floor and crossed himself, invoking the Lord to ward off evil spirits. "Then tell me," his voice rose, "who was crucified? Were the Father and the Holy Spirit not crucified?"

"It was Jesus Christ who was crucified. You are pressing into details that will lead you to blasphemy. The Trinity—the Father, the Son, and the Holy Spirit—together form the Godhead."

The Syrian theologian replied calmly:

"By that definition, there are not one but three Gods. The faith of Moses teaches us that there is but one God. This is written in the Old Testament. And do we not still read that sacred text?"

The scholar from Constantinople could no longer contain his indignation. "Whatever may or may not be written in the Old Testament, you Syrians may have embraced Christianity, but in your heart of hearts, you remain a Jew . . ."

The Syrian scholar lifted his eyes to the ceiling and made the sign of the cross. "Lord God, Holy Father, help us!" He turned back to his accuser. "You dare call a devout Christian a Jew, knowing full well that the Jews thirst for our blood?"

Caesar Justinian rubbed his forehead, his elbow leaning against the armrest of his throne. Seyavash was well-acquainted with the Greek language. He had followed the entire exchange, trying his best to conceal his smile. He was well aware that similar disputes erupted frequently among Christian sects in Ctesiphon. More than once, the Sasanian army had been forced to intervene to keep the peace between them.

Justinian chewed his lip for a few moments. If it were possible, he would never get entangled in this debate, but he had a responsibility. He knew that the task of resolving the rift between the doctrines of oneness and Trinity in the great and sacred Christian faith had fallen to him. Above all, the council of scholars from Constantinople—first assembled by a Roman Caesar—was revered in all of Christendom. Tributes of gold and silver poured in from distant lands, and their coffers rivaled those of the emperor himself. In times of need, it was they who extended the King a loan at a modest interest rate. At last, he gripped his staff, and spoke sternly to the Syrian theologian:

"In my judgment, your exegesis is faulty. Do not sow division within the faith. The Holy Scriptures have been translated into Latin, yet most of you lack the ability to read them properly. You may take your leave."

The court ushers escorted the Syrian theologians out. As they departed, they muttered among themselves, their hardened expressions leaving no doubt that they would not relent from their cause so easily.

Next, Justinian turned to the theologians from Constantinople and addressed them in Latin. He was keenly aware that there were only a handful of people left in Constantinople who still spoke Latin fluently. The empire had come to be so deeply influenced by the Greek tradition that Latin had faded into the recesses of memory. But he took great pride in his command of Latin. He seized the moment to display his knowledge before the theologians.

"Perhaps this matter can only be settled with the edge of a sword," Justinian declared. "But most of these people dwell beyond the boundaries of Rome. We will not permit them to propagate their ideas in our kingdom. You have my word."

The scholars from Constantinople looked at the Caesar with grateful smiles.

"We shall take our leave now," they said.

The Caesar nodded, then added: "And see to it that a copy of the book of Roman law is prepared for a scholar well-versed in Latin. I intend to compile a complete code of Roman law in Latin, titled *Corpus Juris Civilis*. In accordance with Roman law, the official religion of the Roman empire shall be the Trinitarian faith. Henceforth, only those who profess Christianity shall be granted Roman citizenship."

The faces from Constantinople lit up.

"Very good!" exclaimed one of them. "At last, we shall be rid of those cursed Nestorians!"

Caesar Justinian cast a casual glance toward the Sasanian guests. He had heard that their royal scribes spent day and night immersed in the drafting of civil law.

The delegation of scholars prepared to take their leave. Suddenly, a thought occurred to the Caesar—the Old Testament. Its study could not be forbidden. He addressed the delegation again:

"One more thing: review the sacred texts of the Old Testament. See if certain amendments might be made to render them more appropriate for Christians."

"The Jews will make a fuss," a scholar replied with a smile.

"We shall not leave them in any position to do so," remarked Justinian.

Once the delegation of theologians had departed, Justinian exhaled deeply and turned to face the Sasanian guests.

"Welcome to Constantinople!" he greeted them with open arms.

"I received your message. Let me say this, commander: though there is no formal peace treaty between Rome and the Sasanid empire, I do not wish to disappoint you, nor to send you away empty-handed. Tomorrow morning, after a ceremonial exchange of arms, I will grant my protection to the deposed prince. But . . ." he paused for a moment, and added thoughtfully, "I cannot commit to any written agreement at the moment."

Seyavash considered the emperor's words.

"We will accept these terms for now," he said at last. "But tell me, will our crown prince at least be safe here?"

"You need not worry," the Caesar assured Seyavash. "He shall be safe and will be well-cared for. He will live the life of a Roman noble. Now go. Rest."

Justinian gave a slight nod, signaling that the audience had come to an end. The ushers led the Aryan guests to the bedchambers in the royal guest wing. As they walked, Seyavash noticed that the carpets lining the hallways were perfect replicas of the famed carpets from Shiraz. He smiled discreetly.

In the royal bedchamber, two beds awaited the guests. As they settled in for the night, Prince Khosrow asked Seyavash:

"Will the Romans still attack our kingdom one day?"

Seyavash let out a long breath.

"Who can say?" he replied. "For now, the Roman legions are occupied on the western front. The Caesar is intent on reclaiming all the territories lost to the Western armies."

Khosrow's heart swelled with admiration for the Roman emperor. He liked the Caesar. *An emperor*, he thought, *should be just like Justinian.*

"Does the Caesar come from royal blood?" Khosrow asked thoughtfully.

"Not in the least . . ." replied Seyavash. "His paternal uncle was a general in the Roman army. He ascended to the throne, and then named Justinian his successor. No one in their bloodline had ever worn the crown before him."

"Is that so?" asked Khosrow, a flicker of disappointment in his voice. He had always held Aryan ideals in the highest regard. *Lineage and wealth!* he thought resolutely. *These ideals are the foundations of imperial grandeur.* They impressed the authority of empire on the minds of the subjects. And Mazdak! That lying, lowborn charlatan cloaked in the robes of a mobed from some ordinary fire-temple—he had no regard for both these values . . . he remembered Naindokht's parting words to him:

"*Always side with justice.*"

"I shall rule with justice," Khosrow had promised his mother, taking her hand in his. "But . . ." his voice grew firm. "Justice demands punishment. A king must rule with a stern hand."

Khosrow missed Naindokht with a fierce longing. She was still so beautiful! Khosrow loved his mother dearly. He had heard that there was a time, long ago, when it was lawful for Arya men to marry their own mother and sisters. This preserved the purity of the royal bloodline. But that custom had long since been outdated. Yet even now, preference was still given to the children of both maternal and paternal uncles or aunts to marry the royal heirs.

Absorbed in these thoughts, the young prince drifted off to sleep.

Over the next few days, Seyavash completed the arrangements for the prince and got ready to depart.

* * *

Ctesiphon's nights once again echoed with the sounds of its residents screaming and wailing.

The Bedouins in the surrounding areas near Hirah's borders were launching relentless attacks on the capital. Goshtasp had sent them several messages, insisting that these attacks were no longer necessary, but to no avail. The nobles had even attempted to offer money to the Bedouin tribes in exchange for stopping the attacks, but the Bedouins had begun to enjoy these expeditions. They acquired more wealth from Ctesiphon that they had ever gathered from looting merchant caravans. Since Qobad's banishment, nobles had begun returning to the city, and prosperity flowed through its streets once more. The Roman emperor never refused the Bedouin tribes when they asked for weapons.

"Shake the foundations of the Arya empire," he would say with a smile.

Caesar Justinian was preoccupied with other matters. He was overseeing the compilation and inscription of Roman law, and was laying the foundation of a church so magnificent the likes of which had never been seen in the western Roman empire.

Meanwhile, the Sasanian cavalry was engaged on three fronts at once. The Armenians' treachery showed no signs of abating. At the same time, they faced rebellion from the Jews, who had seized control of the territories surrounding Ctesiphon. And on another front, they were forced to confront the Bedouins of Tanukh in combat.

Who could help the Aryans neutralize the three threats?

Qobad.

This name was once again being whispered among the nobles. Qobad had forged a strong alliance with Munzir, the leader of Hirah, who could tighten the reins on his desert tribes. The

Jews and Christians of the kingdom bore no ill will toward him. Qobad had not only permitted them to practice their religion freely, but had also allowed them to build splendid temples for their worship.

"But . . ." objected the elders, clutching their heads, "Qobad is imprisoned in Mazdak's clutches. What are we to do with this Mazdak!"

* * *

Mazdak was at peace.

The rains had brought glad tidings for the farmers in the region. Most had returned to their lands and were busy building reservoirs to collect the water. His newest supporters were the children of nobles attending schools. They came by the dozens from all corners of the kingdom to visit him in Ctesiphon. With newfound hope, they carefully copied the Prophet's commandments and took them home to distribute across their provinces. During these visits, many suggested that Mazdak journey to their lands himself. Among them was Kavus, Qobad's eldest son.

"Holy Prophet, it is important that you visit the provinces yourself. The people must hear your message directly from you. The truth is, according to our sources, some territories have begun to misconstrue your commandments. There are leaders who refuse to engage in any honest work, and are content with looting and plundering as their way of life."

Mazdak did not refuse Prince Kavus's plea. In his eyes, Kavus was the rightful heir to Qobad's throne. Accompanied by the prince and a group of young followers, he began preparing for his journey across the provinces. Before his departure, he went to visit the former king, Balash. Blinded and in hiding, Balash lived in a haveli near Ctesiphon. The mobeds and nobles had once ordered a hot iron rod to be passed over his eyes, ensuring that he would never again dream of becoming king again.

The old blind man was overjoyed to receive Mazdak. Gingerly reaching out to feel his hands and shoulders, he said:

"If I could, I would take you to my homeland, Makran. To Sibi, and Sijistan. Where there are walled canals, and the dates are sweeter than those in Hirah. Where seven mountains rise high into the sky. Each mountain is ruled by its own chief, and guarded by brave Baloch men dressed in black. I've heard that even the farmers and craftsmen over there now call themselves Mazdakites. But I . . . I have gone blind." Tears welled in his eyes.

"Lord Balash," said Mazdak, his voice thick with sorrow, "the cruelty the mobeds and nobles have inflicted upon you will not go unpunished. They are a crumbling power. I may not be able to go to Makran myself, as it lies on the far edge of the kingdom, but I will certainly send someone to bring you dates from there." With a heavy heart, Mazdak departed.

A few days later, accompanied with Prince Kavus and his companions, Mazdak left Ctesiphon with the intent of journeying to Istakhr. When Goshtasp received word of Mazdak's departure, he urged King Jamasp to command the cavalry to finish off the Mazdakites.

"I cannot command a massacre," the King refused bluntly.

"But lord king! Their mischief-making is becoming insufferable. We should reopen the fire-temples and immediately start restocking them with supplies. They have converted many fire-temples into private residences for craftsmen. Their excuse? Homelessness. These wretched people have even turned a few of the fire-temples into caravanserais for villagers passing through. The mobeds are losing their livelihoods, Your Highness."

"That is very unfortunate," said Jamasp evenly.

"What are your orders, your majesty?" Goshtasp asked, leaning forward eagerly.

"I believe it would be suitable to pardon them," the King replied calmly. "And advise them to change their ways. We shall withdraw an appropriate sum from the royal treasury to support this effort."

"The royal coffers? They are nearly depleted, lord . . ." Goshtasp said hesitantly.

"Then collect the money from the nobles," Jamasp replied without pause.

The nobles warned Goshtasp against a genocide of the Mazdakites.

"The farmers will stop working the land. They may take up arms against our troops. You know as well as anyone that farmers march with the troops in all important battles, and have had extensive military training."

"That was our gravest mistake!"

The nobles exchanged uneasy looks, rubbing their hands in regret.

* * *

In the Abdali Khanate, Qobad was getting busier by the day. He had pledged to the Khan that once he reclaimed his throne, he would pay a reasonable tribute to the Khan and his people. He had also grown fond of the Abdali princess—his new wife. She was unlike the Sasanian women—tall, and an expert horsewoman and fighter. She spent most of her time with her first husband, an important general in the Khan's army.

"Jeet Khan and I have sword fighting contests," Princess Sera told Qobad.

Jeet Khan received Qobad with warmth and enthusiasm. They embraced each other. He was a stalwart, fearless Abdali.

"I am raising one thousand troops for you," he told Qobad. "And I shall lead them myself. The Khan has appointed me commander-in-chief of this army, which will crush the Sasanian cavalry and help you reclaim your throne."

Qobad studied Jeet Khan with admiration in his eyes. He felt he could completely trust him.

But Naindokht had not taken to the Abdalis, nor did she get along with Qobad's new wife. In her judgement, Sera was more like a man than a woman, despite her striking beauty.

Naindokht was counting the days until she could return home.

Each day after military training, Seyavash and his men mingled with the Abdalis. They spent long hours on their vast pastures tending to their horses. Every year, they took a fresh caravan of horses to Khotan for trade, where the nobles rewarded them with silks, gold and silver ornaments, intricately crafted dishes studded with diamonds, sapphires, and rubies, and sumptuous carpets. The Abdali camps glittered with these treasures.

CHAPTER 33

In a time of chaos and confusion, when none remained to care for the Sasanian kingdom, when bridges over rivers and streams crumbled with no one to repair them, when the streets and alleyways of Ctesiphon were in need of cleaning because laborers had stopped receiving wages in accordance with Mazdakite law, and when daily life was caught between old codes and new, Joshwa fell in love.

He first met slim, slender, delicate Farkhanda at the edge of a broken wooden bridge over the Tigris. Both were waiting for a canoe to take them across the river. A conversation began while they waited. Farkhanda had recognized Joshwa.

"I heard your speech for the farmers and craftsmen," she said, her eyes full of love. "You speak so well . . . every word goes straight to the heart."

Joshwa's heart rejoiced. He had heard farmers, miners, and craftsmen praise him to the skies, just as often as he had heard the biting criticism of mobeds and nobles. But never before had he felt such gladness of the heart at being admired. In just a few moments, they had forgotten all about the canoe.

"Why don't we swim across the river?" Joshwa suggested.

Farkhanda laughed. "But I don't know how to swim. Since when do the women of Ctesiphon learn swimming!"

Joshwa was deep in thought. *What if this girl is Zoroastrian?* From her clothes and manner, she didn't seem to be. *I hope she's Jewish,* he prayed.

But how could he find out? It would be rude to inquire about someone's religion the first time they were meeting.

"I can escort you home," he said at last. "Where do you live?"

"Across the river, in the Christian settlement," replied Farkhanda.

Oh no! Joshwa thought ruefully. *So she's Christian.* But he pushed the doubt from his heart. *We are all Mazdakites now.* He reminded himself. *If she truly likes me, she must know I've played a role in establishing the true religion in this kingdom.*

Mustering his courage, he asked: "You do believe in the one true religion, don't you?"

Farkhanda couldn't help but laugh. Looking straight into Joshwa's eyes, she said: "My family follows the Trinitarian faith." Then, she smiled and crossed herself.

But the revelation did not faze Joshwa. He was utterly in love with her. In the boat, she sat close beside him. After they had crossed the river, Joshwa walked her home.

It was a respectable home with traditional Christian values. Farkhanda's father and older brother were physicians, and great admirers of Jalinus.

When he returned home, Joshwa relayed everything to his father.

"Honorable father . . . but the girl . . . she's Christian."

Joshwa's elderly father fell silent. After a long pause, he said:

"We should convert to Christianity," he finally said.

Joshwa was stunned.

"What are you saying? But we . . . Father, I am a Mazdakite!"

"Don't be foolish!" Joshwa's mother said gently. "Listen to your father. He is giving you wise council."

"In light of the kingdom's present circumstances—which my eyes can still clearly at this age—it will soon become impossible for us to continue living in the Sasanian empire. Every day, while you're out, we wait with our hearts in our throats. Mazdakites are being hunted—it has become routine to find them and kill them when they are alone. Their dead bodies are turning up in dark corners. We will convert. You will marry this girl. And then we will migrate to Rome. Under the Caesar's new laws, we will be granted citizenship."

Joshwa listened to his father in disbelief. His entire life passed before his eyes, but one moment lingered above the rest—a beautiful girl, sitting beside him on a little boat, holding on to his arm with great confidence as she stepped onto the shore.

They were married within a few days. A pastor from a church in the Christian settlement baptized Joshwa and his family, anointing them with holy water and formally converting them from Jews to Trinitarian Christians. At Joshwa's father's insistence, the newlyweds departed for Constantinople before Mazdak's anticipated arrival in Ctesiphon. Joshwa's parents hoped that the couple would find peace and contentment in Rome, and that, before long, they would be blessed with grandchildren.

"You should write books in Constantinople," Farkhanda advised. "You know Latin, and I've heard that they're doing a great deal of translation work there."

Joshwa's father sold his house and belongings for a modest sum. Torn between the overwhelming sorrow of leaving their homeland behind and the hope of beginning anew, the family bid farewell to the Sasanian kingdom—forever. They were confident that with their new Greek names, they would not be recognized in Constantinople.

* * *

In a paradisiacal garden in Istakhr, Mazdak took part in a debate arranged by his delegation. Though Istakhr's fire-temple was closed, the city's mobed still attended the debate, leaning on his gilded staff.

The garden was thronged with laborer and miners. Two mobeds and two Mazdakites had been appointed as judges for the contest.

Istakhr's mobed stepped forward and raised his staff.

"Our faith and kingdom are crumbling," he began. "Chaos surrounds us. Deprived of lineage and wealth, farmers have turned to looting and plunder. These acts of sacrilege must end, or we shall be erased from the pages of history."

The crowd remained unmoved. Only a handful of scribes seated in the back—no longer allowed to sit in the front rows—clapped happily.

Then Mazdak stepped onto the wooden stage.

"Beloved friends!" he began. "The kingdom is crumbling because the rightful king has been banished. His minor brother has been crowned king, though he has no desire to rule. King Qobad's just laws have been abolished. O citizens of this land, followers of the Mazdakite faith!" he continued, his voice resolute. "Our trials will pass. We have received news that King Qobad is returning with a mighty army. Many among the Sasanian cavalry will join him and fight by his side. As for the mobeds—they shall soon reap what they have sown. They have strayed from the Mazdakite path. Each one of them knows their only concern is the accumulation of wealth. Prepare yourselves to stand with King Qobad."

A ripple of excitement ran through the crowd.

"Zindabad! Zindabad! Long live King Qobad!" The garden reverberated with slogans.

The judges readily announced the results: "Mazdak is the winner of this debate."

The crowd erupted with joy. Their shouts echoed through the garden as they hoisted Mazdak on their shoulders. A few of them went off in search of the city's mobed, sticks in hand, hoping to give him a sound beating. But sensing the mood of the crowd, the mobed had already fled the scene.

Mazdak spent the night in a farmer's humble home. The farmer and his family were beside themselves with happiness. *The Prophet has entered our home!* they thought. Nobles had sent trays heaped with rich, delicious food, but Mazdak sent them back.

"We do not partake in meat," he said humbly.

"We don't eat meat either, Honored Prophet!" the farmer's wife laughed through her tears. "Where would we get enough dirhams to afford meat!"

The Prophet took supper with the farmer's family on an old, tattered *dastarkhwan*. Yogurt, onions, and freshly baked naan from the oven outside the hut. Grain flowed abundantly in their home now. Their children played with plush silk pillows they had taken from a haveli. The Prophet suddenly thought of Azar Barzin—his beloved Kurd disciple—whose house he used to visit regularly. *Where would he be right now?*

The next day, Mazdak left with Prince Kavus for a debate in another province.

Accompanied with the mighty Abdali warriors, Qobad prepared to depart. Precisely at that moment, Seyavash arrived with an urgent message from Ctesiphon.

Scrawled on woven straw pages was a brief message marked with the nobles' seal:

"O sovereign of both worlds, exalted majesty, most munificent lord!

"Your splendid empire, unrivaled in both the earthly and heavenly realms, that strikes terror in the hearts of envious foes and brings death upon them, we, your devoted nobles seek to return your kingdom to you—heart and soul—and spare you the burden of an invasion. We would count ourselves most fortunate to be granted the honor of kissing your feet.

"O sagacious king, we implore you to ascend the throne once more and rid the Sasanian crown of Mazdak's curse, which has cast the realm into despair."

Seyavash's face lit up with joy.

"Do not act in haste, lord king!" he said to Qobad with a smile. "Counsel would be prudent."

Qobad placed the letter before the Khan.

"Very good!" the Khan declared. "My cherished son-in-law, you must go. This does not appear to be a trap. My spies have reported that your kingdom has truly fallen into ruin, and the idea of restoring you to the throne is being discussed openly in the palaces of Ctesiphon. Still, as a precaution, the Abdali army shall accompany you."

A flower-adorned Ctesiphon welcomed Qobad.

In the palace garden, Prince Khosrow stood waiting. Naindokht's eyes glittered at the sight of her son—now a grown man, striking and noble in appearance. Khosrow fell at his mother's feet.

"Being apart from you felt like spending life in hell," he said.

Then he bowed before Qobad in reverent obeisance. The King looked upon his son with pride. In that moment, he resolved to name Khosrow the crown prince.

CHAPTER 34

Why is this door so high?

Prophet Mazdak wondered this as he stepped into the royal palace and walked into the great hall. *Such lofty architecture make man seem so small.* That must be the purpose of towering structures—to make man feel reduced and insignificant.

He had come to visit Qobad. A horde of his disciples stood outside the colossal archway. They never left his side now. But only the Prophet was permitted to enter. Seyavash accompanied him, leaving his rider outside the palace gates. To reach the King, they navigated winding corridors and pathways that they had never walked before. But today, Mazdak was not meeting the King in secret. A prophet was visiting a king in broad daylight. Both king and prophet had helped each other; each had saved the other's life. Since then, Mazdak's name had echoed through the kingdom and beyond its borders. Today, he walked with conviction in his steps.

Seyavash beamed with joy. He was a bridge between king and prophet—both dear to him from the depths of his heart.

The King rose to his full height to welcome them into his chamber.

"Welcome, beloved prophet!" he said, arms outstretched.

"And a hundred thousand times over—welcome, my king!" Mazdak smiled and bowed his head.

At that very moment, Prince Khosrow entered the room. With bold, purposeful strides, he walked over and stood near them.

Qobad placed a hand on Khosrow's shoulder and proudly turned to Mazdak, as though presenting a great triumph.

"Khosrow . . . the Prophet!"

"Welcome, my prince," said Mazdak.

But in contrast to the three smiling faces in the room, Prince Khosrow wore a grave expression. As soon as his gaze fell on Seyavash, his eyes darkened. Despite being royalty, he called Seyavash "uncle" in private. Seyavash had saved his life, had delivered him safely to the Roman empire, which had shaped him into the strong, commanding figure he now was. What a tragedy that the burdens of governing an empire left no room for sentiment. For now, however, royal proclamations were being issued to announce Seyavash's appointment as the new commander-in-chief of the Sasanian cavalry. Though the decrees still bore the nobles' seals, they could not be finalized until the King had signed them—only then could the nobles affix their seals in turn. Prince Khosrow had taken all these seals into his own custody. In his waning years, Qobad often felt that the vigor of Khosrow's youth had come into full bloom.

They settled into ornate Roman chairs and began their conversation.

Mazdak longed to express his happiness about the King's return. He had heard the rumors that the nobles were plotting to drive a wedge between him and the King. But he remained hopeful that once Prince Kavus ascended to the throne, his and his disciples' burdens would be lifted.

"I visited Istakhr with the crown prince, Your Highness," Mazdak said earnestly.

"Crown prince?" Qobad asked, visibly surprised.

"Prince Kavus," Mazdak replied with certitude.

"Oh!" said Qobad. "He hasn't come to greet me yet."

"He is on his way to Ctesiphon from Tabaristan, Your Majesty!" Mazdak assured Qobad. "Rushing from province to province, eager to fall at your feet."

"Prophet," Khosrow said solemnly. "We have not received good news from Tabaristan. The nobles' estates over there are being looted day and night."

"You have been misinformed," Mazdak replied. "Our enemies exaggerate in order to sow discord. Only those orders are being enforced which bear His Majesty's seal. And if there have been any injustices, they have been swiftly remedied."

Mazdak went on to extol Ahura Mazda and the one true faith, but Prince Khosrow was no longer listening.

On his way to Ctesiphon . . .

The words echoed in Khosrow's mind. *But where, exactly?*

That night, in the King's bedchamber, Naindokht sat beside the King, her hand resting gently on his shoulder. The King signed the royal proclamation declaring Prince Khosrow as the crown prince. He pressed his seal into the wax and handed the document to his son. As was the custom, three copies of the edict were to be prepared and dispatched to three senior judges across the realm. These sealed proclamations could only be opened upon Qobad's death—they were his final will, the unalterable testament to his legacy.

"Good night, my Nosherwan . . . O immortal soul. Be just." Naindokht whispered, kissing her son's cheeks. It was Prince

Khosrow who had entered the room, but it was Nosherwan the Just who emerged.

Kingship demands a resolute heart, my beautiful, gentle mother! his heart called out to Naindokht. *But how could she ever understand? I shall tell her only stories of my justice.*

That very night, before the first blush of dawn, Prince Kavus and his companions perished in a fateful ambush.

Busy Qobad!

The Jewish communities welcomed his envoys warmly. They saw that King Qobad's return had revived unity in the Sasanian cavalry, and they were tired of the Seven Years' War. The final matter at hand was the disagreement over the proclamations calling for the restoration of the Jews' religious freedom and former privileges. The King's sole condition was that the Jews resume service in the Sasanian cavalry, just as they had in the past. He was already more than satisfied with their tax collection and stewardship of the royal coffers.

To rein in the rebellious Tanukh tribes, Qobad needed the Roman Caesar's support. The Tanukhids' insatiable greed for gold had already stripped them of their standing with Hirah's leader, Munzir.

This secluded Arab state had seen many try to oust Munzir. What really mattered was disrupting the flow of weapons from Constantinople to the Tanukhid tribes. As for Emperor Justinian, he, too, was as absorbed in affairs of state as King Qobad. He had his sights set westward—toward Constantinople itself.

CHAPTER 35

I shall leave my name upon the pages of history, Justinian vowed.

He believed it was the will of Lord God himself that he restore the Roman empire to its former glory. His brave warriors had conquered Hispania and driven out the rogue Goth tribes and Vandals. Many had converted to Christianity and pledged their loyalty to him, and the rest wandered aimlessly by the seashore. Religious solidarity was paramount for the empire's survival, yet Justinian found himself ensconced in a raging conflict: Was the Lord Jesus Christ one, or two? Was he human, or divine? This dispute seemed to have no end in sight. Only the priests of Constantinople came forward to help him.

"Verily, two natures are united in the one person of Christ," the pastors assured him. "One who worked miracles, and another who was human and suffered injury—he who died on the cross. If the two natures were truly one person, does it not follow that God died on the cross, and if so . . . how does the world go on without Him?"

The argument had merit. And the Holy Spirit was yet another aspect among these—it wasn't two, it was three of them.

"Yes. Three . . . three of them!" the priests affirmed.

"We shall debate this no further," declared Justinian, striking his gilded gavel sharply against the table.

He had also resolved to purge the Roman empire of Greek philosophers, who were bent on inventing new riddles for them to unravel. Some had fled to Egypt; others sought refuge in the Sasanian kingdom. The truth was, he was weary of the Greek imprint on the Christian kingdom. What he longed for was a revival of Latin—his mother tongue, and surely, he believed, the language of Christianity as well. Or at the very least, it ought to be. But few people spoke or understood Latin anymore, which made it all the more formidable—whereas Greek was commonly known, even among the fishmongers of Constantinople. And yet, anything communicated in Latin carried a natural air of sophistication.

Emperor Justinian had begun the construction of a magnificent church in Constantinople. Once, a Greek orthodox church had stood on the same ground, its name synonymous with "The Wisdom of God." The Greek word for wisdom was *sophia*—and what was wisdom? Another Greek word—*logos*. It vexed Justinian that everything had already been written in the Greek language. *Alas! Latin is not a language of many words*, he lamented.

The priests of his parish explained that wisdom is best revealed through dialogue. And so, what follows, is the word.

"In the beginning was the Word, and the Word was with God, and . . ."

"And what?" asked Justinian.

"And the Word was God. What else could it be, Your Majesty?"

Then, they sketched a mathematical theorem on a piece of paper—the atheist Euclid himself might have envied it.

It was a triangle, with another triangle inscribed within it, and at the center, a circle. Written inside the circle in plain letters was: *God.*

The outer triangle stated:

The Father = not The Son
The Son = not The Holy Spirit
The Holy Spirit = not The Father

The inner triangle stated:

The Father = God
The Son = God
The Holy Spirit = God

"Is the matter clear now?" the senior priest inquired curiously.

The matter was anything but clear to Justinian, but in his judgement, one fact was unmistakable: he would require a substantial sum of money to build his church. Could he levy new taxes across the Roman empire?

"Not likely," opined his chief treasurer.

So much of the empire's wealth was being funneled into military expeditions on the western front that the royal treasury was nearly depleted.

So, when Qobad's envoys arrived, bearing a message of gratitude from the Sasanian king for safeguarding the crown prince, the Caesar brightened.

"What standing do the Tanukh tribes even have? We won't grant them so much as an arrow or a dagger. Come—let us enter into a peace treaty; one that shall last forever!"

The Sasanian envoys leapt for joy. Was it really possible?

"The only condition is that King Qobad offer five hundred pounds in weight of gold to the Roman empire. We shall sign the treaty without delay."

The envoys' faces fell.

"Lord Caesar! Our kingdom is steeped in troubles of its own," they began, but then they stopped. It would not be prudent to disclose every secret of the kingdom before this enemy-like friend . . . or friend-like enemy.

"We shall deliver your message, and make every effort to arrange the gold for this eternal peace. But you must assure us that the Tanukh tribes will no longer attack us, Your Majesty."

"As of today," the Caesar pledged. His viziers nodded along vigorously.

Bearing the message of hope, the Sasanian delegation departed for their homeland. One thing bewildered them about the Roman empire—the staggering number of rats scurrying about within the palace walls. According to their faith, rats had been created by Ahriman. Did that mean that Ahriman was gaining power over the capital city of this glorious empire?

* * *

One of the envoys reached Mazdak bearing a letter from Constantinople. It was from his dear friend Joshwa:

> It grieves me that I could not see you before my departure, and now, we find ourselves here—in a glittering city crowded with slaves. Most of them are the sons and daughters of farmers. They work on landed estates, and when they fail to repay debts owed to

landowners, they are taken in bondage and sold in slave auctions. Their children are born into servitude. Some are made eunuchs while still young, to serve in the homes of the wealthy, havelis of the nobility, and even in the royal palace.

On the outskirts of this resplendent city lie the settlements of the poor, with entire families packed into single rooms. As an act of kindness, Roman elites distribute rounds of flatbread among them. One poorhouse belongs to the emperor. Fights are quick to erupt in these poorhouses, and the city's armed guards often have to quell the disturbance with lashes. Among them, many are eventually sold into slavery, having failed to repay their debts.

We have a house on the west side of the city. I live there with my wife, her father, and her brothers. Just yesterday, my father-in-law purchased two slaves from the market. One was a boy, sold for ten nomisma—roughly equal to ten Sasanian dinars. The other, a young man, cost him twenty dinars. Eunuchs, children, and able-bodied adults fetch higher prices. Some among them are prisoners of war, but they do not speak the language.

My beloved friend and teacher—I have resolved to bring your message first to the slaves, and through them, to the laborers and workers of Constantinople.

A grave affliction haunts the city—the plague has broken out, and each day, the poor perish in large numbers. My father-in-law and brothers-in-law are physicians. Day and night, they move through the poor settlements, tending to the sick. Sometimes, I accompany them.

My dear friend, I have received word that the death toll among the farmers is much higher than that of city folk. In the farms, corpses are falling by the hundreds on a daily basis. Despite the rising number of deaths, the emperor and his men refuse to lower taxes by so much as half a dirham, and extract the full tax as they whip the dying farmers. It seems that soon, the number of enslaved farmers will rise, as the Roman Caesar will need them; he is raising a splendid church in the memory of their prophet, Jesus Christ. It confounds the mind that a king who metes out such cruelty upon the weak builds a monument to mercy in the name of Jesus!

We shall come to see you soon—if we live.

Your eternal friend,
Joshwa

"Eternity!" Mazdak echoed. "A time period unknown."

CHAPTER 36

"Eternity!" Qobad repeated gaily. "Who has ever seen such a thing? But what an excellent idea—eternal peace with the Roman empire!"

Engrossed in his worrying thoughts, Qobad wondered how he would pay five hundred pounds of gold. He could ask his Abdali friends for help, but all they had were thoroughbred warhorses, and battle-hardened horsemen—no gold.

"Shall we put pressure on the mobeds and nobles?" the King asked his son. Qobad had been ill lately.

"I would advise against it," Khosrow Nosherwan said to his father. "We have just regained control over the kingdom. It wouldn't be wise to offend the scholars and nobles. My honorable father, leave this matter to me. You have been working tirelessly the past few days. You really need to get some rest."

Qobad smiled and looked at his son contentedly. In a few days' time, he departed for Istakhr with Naindokht to spend some time in his opulent royal palace.

* * *

Qobad had this red-stone palace built for himself and Naindokht with great devotion by the banks of the River Karkhah. But until tonight, circumstances hadn't allowed him to spend a single moment looking upon the crescent moon in peace. Now that he was here with Naindokht at last, his fever was not letting go. Nevertheless, he felt content and serene. He sat with Naindokht in a vast meadow next to the river, his eyes fixed on a white ship anchored to the shore. It bobbed gently on the waves, as if it were sailing. As soon as they saw the King and queen, the grazing deer leapt and hid behind the trees. Whenever a gust of wind turned the branches, they would catch a glimpse of their big eyes, or their soft, twitching ears. A mill was spinning slowly in the distance, and the laborers pouring bags of grain and carrying bags of ground flour on their backs looked like busy dwarves. Qobad studied them keenly.

"I hope they are no longer starving," he said in a voice barely above a whisper.

"Not at all, my king! Light of my eyes," Naindokht consoled him. "The famine is over, and they receive their full wages now."

Qobad suddenly remembered Mazdak. Where was he at the moment? *He saved my life and my kingdom.*

Taking Naindokht's hand in his, he said: "Tell Khosrow not to be too harsh on Mazdak."

"Why are you talking like this, Your Highness? You are the sovereign of the kingdom. Upon your return, you can have a detailed conversation with Mazdak yourself."

Qobad smiled.

"Let's go inside," he said, and hoisted himself up with one hand on Naindokht's shoulder for support.

The maidservants doubled over and made their obeisances:

"Would you like to take supper, Your Majesty?"

Cold and hot meats, fragrant rice simmered in olive oil, succulent chicken fed on opium seed, its meat tender and its flavor intoxicating, and halwas laced with pistachios and almonds.

"No . . ." Qobad smiled faintly. Naindokht's worry deepened at once. Scabs had begun to form on his lips. She led him to his bedchamber, where the royal physicians and their assistants were hastily summoned. One physician offered the King a carefully prepared tonic to ease the bitterness of his medicines. Handkerchiefs of fine cotton, soaked in perfumed ice-water, were rubbed gently over his feet, forehead, and face.

Qobad turned onto his side on the soft, silken royal bed and gestured toward his gold-and-pearl armband.

"Give this to our Astrologer," he murmured to Naindokht, who stood at his side like a statue, tears spilling down her cheeks.

Sometime in the night, Qobad breathed his last.

Two riders had departed on lightning-swift horses earlier that evening to deliver the news to the capital.

Khosrow Nosherwan's day had been consumed with nerve-wracking matters. He had not emerged from his bedchamber except for breakfast and supper. Yet, news of every passing moment reached him.

CHAPTER 37

The proclamation naming Seyavash as commander-in-chief had been delayed. The King had departed for Istakhr before affixing his seal, and the nobles had raised grave objections about the appointment. Seyavash was to appear before the judge today—this was the day his fate would be sealed.

"Are you firm upon the Zoroastrian faith?"

"Yes, Your Honor."

"But your wife died only recently. You did not have her laid upon the dokhma. You had her buried!"

"That is not unheard of, Your Honor. I am but a soldier. There have even been Sasanian kings who have preferred burial."

"Did your wife prefer a burial? Was it her will and testament? If so, do you have any proof?"

"I have made no such claim, Your Honor."

"Then you buried a Zoroastrian woman in the worthless dust without her permission? Like the Christians and Jews?"

Seyavash was quiet. He would not say that dust, too, was sacred—he did not want to drag Mazdak's true religion into the court.

"And have you not begun to worship new deities?"

"No, Your Honor."

"Such as the deity of good fortune?"

"That deity already belongs to the sacred Zoroastrian faith, Your Honor."

"Does it not contradict Mani?"

The judges' pens moved across the parchment.

"Seyavash is a heretic. He must be put to death."

A message from Khosrow:

Put a dagger through his heart and finish him. The body must not be mutilated. With all due reverence, his intact body is to be laid upon the dokhma on the royal hill at the break of dawn.

"Farewell, dear uncle," Khosrow murmured under his breath. "Your two friends brought ruin to the Sasanian empire. And you . . . you could never part ways with them."

CHAPTER 38

No significant obstacle stood in the way of Khosrow Nosherwan's coronation. A minor plot surfaced, but the King's army quickly quashed it.

The Sasanian king himself composed a letter to invite the shahs of all the provinces to the crowning. The letter was a perfect satire—Khosrow began by expressing grief over his father's passing, but in such a way that the intended meaning behind the words was obvious.

"After the customary pleasantries, let it be clear that nothing strikes fear in people's hearts like the death of a king whose ineffectual presence provokes disorder, and brings down one misery after another—upon good people, upon their servants, upon their wealth, and upon everything they hold dear. We do not consider anything to be as harmful for the people as the death of a good king . . ."

After reading the letter, the nobles breathed a sigh of relief and smiled. The chief mobed wrapped his long, red silk cloak around him, stroked his beard, and said to Goshtasp:

"Make no mistake—Khosrow will not grant us any of our former privileges. He is even more stubborn than his father."

Goshtasp exhaled deeply. "At least he won't seize our lands and property. Let us be content for now."

At the center of the capital, River Tigris flowed mightily. At the bank of the Sarsar canal that emerged from the river was Mazdak, walking slowly in his long cloak, a throng of thousands of his disciples following close behind on the wide road.

The flock consisted of farmers and miners from remote villages, tailors from the city, schoolteachers, sweepers and trash collectors, cobblers and potters.

On the eastern bank of the canal was the capital's grandest church. The towering white structure was visible from miles away. A monastery sat next to the church, with one hundred rooms reserved as residences for monks. Today, Mazdak was taking part in a debate with these monks.

In the distance, a chariot drawn by four horses approached them at lightning speed. Mazdak's companions quickened their steps and moved closer to the edge of the bank, making way for the oncoming chariot.

"He is right ahead of me," a noble aboard the chariot said, even though he was still a short distance away from the crowd.

"If I wish it, my arrow could pierce his chest this instant."

"No!" his companion stilled his hand. "Not like this. We'll follow the law."

The chariot raced past the throng, raising a cloud of dust in its wake. Mazdak stepped down to wash his face and hands. His companions likewise washed the dust off their faces. They decided to stop and rest for a while. They opened the bundles they were carrying on their shoulders and sat down to eat onions, cucumbers, and naan.

Reciting the Avesta, Mazdak put the first morsel in his mouth.

"Will we ever . . ." a sweeper began hesitantly. "Will we ever be able to ride in chariots, venerable prophet?"

Mazdak studied him. "Why not?" he replied. "Ten to twelve people can easily ride in one of these. They have not been made for one or two nobles."

"There are so many chariots in Ctesiphon that all of us will get to ride in them," said a tailor, cracking his knuckles.

"And nobles are returning to Ctesiphon each day with at least four chariots in tow," added a miner. "Prophet, you no longer permit us, otherwise seizing these chariots and what's aboard them is a matter of moments."

"No," Mazdak shook his head. "Grain is a different matter—take it from them. As for everything else . . ." he paused. "We shall convince them."

Mazdak's fellows began to whisper among themselves. They had faith in their prophet's eloquence. They had their own priests appointed in each neighborhood, and could only act on their instructions. And among them was their Prophet Mazdak, whom none could rival in discourse. But they also felt disheartened—their beloved King Qobad had passed on, and their prophet's dearest friend and commander Seyavash had been sentenced to death. Riots had broken out in the city, but fizzled out. The dead were gone, and couldn't be brought back by setting fire to the nobles' havelis. They no longer had the support of the Sasanian cavalry. The disturbances died down. The armies guarding the nobility's private lands had begun to reproach them harshly. But they had not given up hope.

CHAPTER 39

When Mazdak received his invitation from the royal palace to take part in a formal debate, he did not know that the event would be held in the King's privy chamber, not in open court. Announcements had already been made throughout the city that morning that the most able scholars of the Sasanian kingdom would be taking part in a debate today at the Taq Kisra—the Arch of Ctesiphon—against a person who had begun to claim that he was a prophet. But the common people did not receive invitations to attend. What did happen in Ctesiphon in the early hours of the morning was that with great respect, the armed king's guard ushered all of Mazdak's priests into carriages drawn by two horses, and took them to the King's palace.

"They are the only ones who have been allowed to attend and enjoy the debate," the guards told anyone that asked.

The city was emptied of Mazdak's priests. All of them had been taken to the royal palace.

As soon as he walked through the archway, the King's guard surrounded Mazdak and took him to the royal chamber.

The King's chamber dazzled with light. On each gilded chair sat an accomplished scholar and debater. Some of the most powerful nobles in the kingdom were seated grandly upon a wooden stage covered with rich, heavy carpets, including the sons of Mahdad, Niv Shapur, Azar Farrobag, Azar Buz, Azar Mehr, and Bakht Afrid. Not only were they taking part in the contest, but they were also the judges on behalf of the crown.

"But what about my judges?" inquired Mazdak. "Where are they?"

"They will be here any moment," the King's mace-bearers consoled him.

As soon as Khosrow Nosherwan stepped into the room, everyone in the King's court rose to their full height, their eyes and heads lowered in deference. Mazdak was the only one to lock eyes with the King.

Nosherwan smiled bitterly, and took a seat on his throne, leaning against a bolster pillow.

"Begin!" he gestured with his hand.

One after another, religious spokespeople tore Mazdak's teachings apart. The speakers also included representatives of Judaism and Christianity.

The debates continued.

"You! You have only brought ruin to the Sasanian empire. Today, the veil of dignity and honor has been lifted. We have people who neither have inherited property, nor profession, nor skill. Farmers are revolting, breaking into the nobility's palaces, ransacking their homes, seizing their lands. Such is the state of wretchedness in the realm that there is no other choice but to give these heretics the worst punishment—the nine deaths."

"Death penalty! Death penalty! Death penalty!" the King's court shook with the slogans raised by the nobles.

"King Qobad abolished the death penalty," Mazdak said calmly. "I have a copy of his edicts."

“We have buried those edicts in the garden of Taq Kisra. Would you like to see them?” Khosrow Nosherwan himself addressed Mazdak.

The King’s troops seized Mazdak by the arms and led him into the great garden behind the palace.

For a moment, Mazdak couldn’t believe what he saw. As far as the eye could see, human legs grew from the earth like trees, their feet pointed skyward.

“You wished to turn the world upside down, did you not?” came Goshtasp’s voice. “Behold your priests. How splendid they look upside down. We have grown a forest of them—all for you.”

Mazdak felt the sharp blade of a dagger against the back of his neck. Both his hands had been tied behind his back.

Mazdak saw Khosrow Nosherwan standing before him. He was two finger-lengths taller than Mazdak. He wore a string of real pearls around his neck, and a priceless turban on his head with a white plume.

Now Mazdak no longer harbored any doubt—his death was certain within moments. He thought of his wife, heavy with child.

“Khosrow!” he said without fear. “You will take my life, which is a grave sin. The souls of the unjustly slain are never freed. They drift through the elements for all eternity.”

Khosrow Nosherwan responded with a swing of his mighty arm that, thanks to his precise aim, severed Mazdak’s head from his body. The decapitated head rolled around for a few moments at Nosherwan’s diamond-studded shoes.

Servants rushed in to pick up Mazdak’s head and body from the King’s feet. They took it away.

The participants of the debate left dumbfounded. They couldn’t quite believe that the Mazdakite discord was finally over. For years, in their palaces, their gardens, their banquets and feasts, only one name had fallen upon their ears:

Mazdak, Mazdak, Mazdak!

Wherever they went, he stood before them. To think that even sweepers cleaning filth from the roads had begun to claim themselves their equals.

They had to bury all the bodies before dawn.

Khosrow Nosherwan let out a shaky breath. Then he turned to the nobles and said:

"Your work begins now. Starting tomorrow, you will erase Mazdak's name from the history of this kingdom. There should be no mention of him, nor of his contemptible beliefs. Let no tongue dare utter his name. We have to cast his memory—not him—to the fortress of the forgotten ones. And beware—if ever his name must be spoken, let it be so with scorn. Future generations must not find so much as a trace of his name or his legacy. Tonight, from this moment on, let Mazdak be erased from the memory of man."

With willful, measured steps, Khosrow Nosherwan walked toward his palace. The next morning, he was going to be occupied with work. Bridges must be built, and Ctesiphon's ramparts must be fortified. He was the architect of an empire. Under his reign, lineage and wealth would be safe, and doors to the poorhouses would never close.

The following day, the city was quiet.

Mazdak and his priests had vanished. His followers had gone into hiding in their homes. That afternoon, on a trail surrounded by thick forests, the dust-covered face of a miner was spotted in a small two-wheeled cart heading north of Ctesiphon. His cheeks were streaked with tears, and he was returning to his village with his wife and three daughters.

CHAPTER 40

Time passed.

But where? Where does time go?

To the right or the left? Before us or behind? Above or below?

On a summer morning, a girl slowly descended the stairs of her student hostel next to the college building, hiding a book beneath her stole. She was seventeen or eighteen years old, and dressed in the traditional white uniform of the girls' college. She walked toward the back of the playground. Slipping past the prying eyes of other students, she sat down on a plinth of smooth white stone, pulled out her book, and began to read.

"Today, Europe lives in fear of a demon—Communism."

The girl read the opening sentence. At ten o'clock, she was meeting a boy at a big college in the city. He had loaned her this little book. It was eight o'clock. She still had time.

Time.

If time were measured in months and years, then it had been two thousand years since her people came to these lands. They belonged to the Kamboch tribe, which had first been displaced by the rajas of Hind, but they had successfully returned. In pairs and clusters, they scattered hither and yon. They were teachers and astrologers. They settled down in Hind and came to be known as the most supreme caste and race of teachers and astrologers. Then, a few of them adopted a religion that spread from Arabistan. The followers of this religion began to arrive—on horseback, camelback, and even on foot—to these lush, verdant lands of many rivers and pattering rains. It was these very lands between the two great rivers—Ganga and Jamuna—that the ancestors of this girl had made into their dwelling.

Far to the north lay an island surrounded by a raging sea, inhabited by a few tribes and families. The Romans had already invaded the island, and many of them stayed back and settled there. But their rule was short-lived. The inhabitants of another continent attacked the island and took it under their control. During the Roman occupation, the tribes and families on the island adopted the Christian faith. After the Romans left, the naval armies from colder territories repeatedly attacked the island. Having devastated the region and its inhabitants, most of the invaders settled on the island. The wheel of time went on spinning for centuries until it was impossible to distinguish between them. All mixed together and became followers of the Christian faith.

With time, a kingdom emerged whose merchants and armies set out in their majestic ships, sailing the turbulent waves, to establish their sovereignty. They were so victorious in their endeavors that their empire rivalled the past glory of the Roman and Sasanian kingdoms. The inhabitants of this island first came to be known as Britons, and eventually, the name came to signify the population of all those mixed tribes and families as well as the island itself and all its neighboring territories—Great Britain.

The merchants, armies, and rulers of the British empire colonized this vast subcontinent which came to be known as Hindustan. Then, the girl's ancestors—along with numerous other tribes and families—could stay there no longer. Traveling toward the northwestern territories, they came upon new lands, and eventually settled there.

Now this girl was in a beautiful, clean city situated by a cascading river. It was called Sindhuni, but to this day, it is remembered fondly by the locals as Mehran in memory of that Aryan warrior and commander who crossed the river with his troops, and named the river after his own tribe.

About two hundred farsakh—approximately six hundred miles away—were the ruins of an immense fortress. This was possibly the biggest fortress in the world. Nobody remembered its history, and no one could say who built it, but some believed that thousands of years ago, it had been constructed by the Sasanians who came from Iran. The inhabitants of neighboring villages knew it only as Ranikot. A strange forest stood nearby. It was ancient, and instead of turning to dust, its trees had become fossilized over time. The rare tourist in the area would visit these ruins with great enthusiasm.

The country was under the rule of an army chief. He was a Han—now known as Khan—the title of the Huns, which had become an honorific in the past two thousand years. He might not have been related to the Huns.

Three days ago, in a small house on an old street, a group of students—both boys and girls—met in secret. They were weary of the injustices that besieged them from all sides.

"How long will the reign of power and brute force go on?" said one of them.

"The farmers are living in conditions even more wretched than that of the slaves. In the cities, there is no one to ask after the poor. Things must be changed . . ."

The girl had known the taste of poverty. Her father had passed away when she was just a child, and she had lived the life of an orphan. When one of their companions distributed certain books among the girls and boys, the girl eagerly selected a small volume.

Talking among themselves in low voices, the girls and boys stepped out in a queue. "Things can change. It has happened before in other nations. All the wealth of the rich must be seized and distributed equally among all people."

A boy smiled.

"Equality!" he said.

All heads nodded. "Equality . . ." they repeated in whispers. "The same desire beats in our hearts."

The girl glanced at the inexpensive watch around her wrist.

It was time for her to leave.

As she closed her book, she suddenly caught a glimpse of the author. A dark beard and hair, intelligent eyes, and a cynical smile on his lips . . .

In her mind, something stirred. The author was German. His father had been Christian, but he had once belonged to a Jewish family. He had died over sixty to seventy years ago.

She had never traveled beyond the borders of her homeland, nor had she ever met a European.

Then why did she have this strange feeling—an inexplicable sensation—that she had seen this man somewhere. Seen him closely . . . and he gave her something.

In the image, the eyes looked up at the girl with kindness.

Now his smile no longer seemed cynical to her—there was a hint of recognition in those eyes.

She hurriedly closed the book and put it inside her cloth bag. Taking quick steps, she made her way toward the green wooden door of the girls' college.

EPILOGUE

What happened next?

Mazdak's followers were not completely erased from the world. Many historians are of the opinion that they remained in hiding even after the rise of the Arab conquerors. During the Abbasid Caliphate, Babak Khorramdin—better known as Babak Khorrami—led a mutiny that had the support of the Mazdakites.

Fahmida Riaz (1946–2018) was a pioneering Pakistani writer, poet, translator, and human rights activist. Born in Meerut, British India, and raised in Hyderabad, Sindh, Riaz was a bold political voice who used her writing to challenge societal norms and address issues of social justice, gender, and political repression. A fearless critic of authoritarian regimes, she was involved in the anti-Ayub Khan movement and faced charges of sedition under General Zia's martial law, leading to a period of exile in India. Riaz's literary contributions include several poetry collections, novels, and translations, most notably her translations of Persian and classical Sufi works into Urdu. During her lifetime, she received the Himmett-Hellman Award for Resistance Literature and the Sitara-e-Imtiaz.

Sana R. Chaudhry is a Pakistani-American writer, translator, and researcher known for her contributions to South Asian literature. With a background in the humanities, she has dedicated much of her career to translating works of Urdu literature into English and various literary and cultural projects aimed at preserving and promoting the literary traditions of South Asia. She is the author of *Experiments in Silence: The Urdu Short Story After 1947*, and has translated the works of Fahmida Riaz and Julien Columeau.

The **Armory Square Prize for South Asian Literature in Translation** was created to inspire new directions for translators into English from one of the most diverse, historically complex, and culturally vibrant regions of the world. It awards a talented translator of South Asian literature into English with the publication of their outstanding manuscript.

The prize is groundbreaking. It aims to remedy the stark disparities in literary translation worldwide by cultivating a new generation of literary translators working with South Asian languages. Since the award was launched in 2022, it has heralded storytellers from the Indian Subcontinent and elevated them within the broader literary ecosystem.

OPEN LETTER

Inga Ābele (Latvia)
High Tide
Pilar Adon (Spain)
Of Beasts and Fowls
Katixa Agirre (Spain)
Mothers Don't
Naja Marie Aidt (Denmark)
Rock, Paper, Scissors
Esther Allen et al. (ed.) (World)
The Man Between: Michael Henry Heim & a Life in Translation
Bae Suah (South Korea)
A Greater Music
North Station
Zsófia Bán (Hungary)
Night School: A Reader for Grownups
Juan Goméz Bárcena (Spain)
Not Even the Dead
Rusana Bardarska (Bulgaria)
To Essay
Svetislav Basara (Serbia)
The Cyclist Conspiracy
Lutz Bassman (France)
Black Village
Michal Ben-Naftali (Israel)
The Teacher
Guðbergur Bergsson (Iceland)
Tómas Jónsson, Bestseller
Max Besora (Catalonia)
The Adventures and Misadventures of the Extraordinary and Admirable Joan Orpi, Conquistador and Founder of New Catalonia
The Fake Muse
Jean-Marie Blas de Roblès (World)
Island of Point Nemo
Katarzyna Boni (Poland)
Auroville
Ganbare! Workshops on Dying
Per Aage Brandt (Denmark)
If I Were a Suicide Bomber
Dmitry Bykov (Russia)
VZ: Volodymyr Zelenskyy and the Making of a Nation
Can Xue (China)
Frontier
Mother River
Vertical Motion
Lúcio Cardoso (Brazil)
Chronicle of the Murdered House
Víctor Catala (Catalonia)
A Film (3,000 Meters)
Sergio Chejfec (Argentina)
The Dark
The Incompletes
My Two Worlds
The Planets
Eduardo Chirinos (Peru)
The Smoke of Distant Fires
Aliocha Coll (Spain)
Attila
Nataliya Deleva (Bulgaria)
Four Minutes
Manuela Draeger (France)
Eleven Sooty Dreams
Marguerite Duras (France)
Abahn Sabana David
L'Amour
The Sailor from Gibraltar
Elisa Shua Dusapin (Switzerland)
Pachinko Parlor
Vladivostok Circus
Winter in Sokcho
Jana Egle (Latvia)
Birthday
Mathias Énard (France)
Street of Thieves
Zone
Macedonio Fernández (Argentina)
The Museum of Eterna's Novel
Rubem Fonseca (Brazil)
The Taker & Other Stories
Rodrigo Fresán (Argentina)
The Bottom of the Sky
The Dreamed Part
The Invented Part
Melvill
The Remembered Part

OPEN LETTER

Juan Gelman (Argentina)
Dark Times Filled with Light
Oliverio Girondo (Italy)
Decals: Complete Early Poems
Arnon Grunberg (Netherlands)
Good Men
Tirza
Ha Seong-nan (Korea)
Bluebeard's First Wife
Flowers of Mold
Wafers
Hubert Haddad (France)
Rochester Knockings: A Novel of the Fox Sisters
Gail Hareven (Israel)
Lies, First Person
Johan Harstad (Norway)
The Red Handler
Hwang Jungeun (Korea)
Years and Years
Angel Igov (Bulgaria)
A Short Tale of Shame
Ilya Ilf & Evgeny Petrov (Russia)
The Golden Calf
Jingzhi Zou (China)
Ninth Building
Kang Young-sook (Korea)
Rina
Hristo Karastoyanov (Bulgaria)
The Same Night Awaits Us All
Jan Kjærstad (Norway)
The Conqueror
The Discoverer
Josefine Klougart (Denmark)
One of Us Is Sleeping
Andris Kupriš (Latvia)
Berlin
Carlos Labbé (Chile)
Loquela
The Murmuration
Navidad & Matanza
Spiritual Choreographies
Cezary Łazarewicz (Poland)
Did This Hand Kill?
Lee Soho (Korea)
Catcalling
Jakov Lind (Austria)
Ergo
Landscape in Concrete
Nina Lykke (Norway)
Natural Causes
Andri Snær Magnason (Iceland)
On Time and Water
Andreas Maier (Germany)
Klausen
Lucio Mariani (Italy)
Traces of Time
Sara Mesa (Spain)
Among the Hedges
Un Amor: A Novel
Bad Handwriting
Four by Four
Amanda Michalopoulou (Greece)
Why I Killed My Best Friend
Valerie Miles (World)
A Thousand Forests in One Acorn: An Anthology of Spanish-Language Fiction
Subimal Misra (India)
This Could Have Become Ramayan Chamar's Tale: Two Anti-Novels
Wild Animals Prohibited
Iben Mondrup (Denmark)
Justine
Quim Monzó (Catalonia)
Gasoline
Guadalajara
A Thousand Morons
Why, Why, Why?
Lara Moreno (Spain)
The City
Wolfskin
Giulio Mozzi (Italy)
This Is the Garden
Andrés Neuman (Argentina)
Bariloche
A Father Is Born
Once Upon Argentina

OPEN LETTER

Sensitive Anatomy
The Things We Don't Do
Jóanes Nielsen (Faroe Islands)
The Brahmadells
Madame Nielsen (Denmark)
The Endless Summer
Henrik Nordbrandt (Denmark)
When We Leave Each Other
Asta Olivia Nordenhof (Denmark)
The Easiness and the Loneliness
Wojciech Nowicki (Poland)
Salki
Bragi Ólafsson (Iceland)
The Ambassador
Narrator
The Pets
Kristín Ómarsdóttir (Iceland)
Children in Reindeer Woods
Sigrún Pálsdóttir (Iceland)
Boudoir
Embroidery
History. A Mess.
Diego Trelles Paz (ed.) (World)
The Future Is Not Ours
Ilja Leonard Pfeijffer (Netherlands)
Rupert: A Confession
Jerzy Pilch (Poland)
The Mighty Angel
My First Suicide
A Thousand Peaceful Cities
Rein Raud (Estonia)
The Brother
João Reis (Portugal)
The Devastation of Silence
The Translator's Bride
Fahmida Riaz (Pakistan)
Fortress of the Forgotten Ones
Rainer Maria Rilke (Austria)
Sonnets to Orpheus
Mónica-Ramón Ríos (Chile)
Cars on Fire
Mercè Rodoreda (Catalonia)
Camellia Street
Death in Spring
Garden by the Sea
The Selected Stories of Mercè Rodoreda
War, So Much War
Milen Ruskov (Bulgaria)
Thrown into Nature
Remigiusz Ryziński (Poland)
Foucault in Warsaw
Guillermo Saccomanno (Argentina)
77
The Clerk
Gesell Dome
Juan José Saer (Argentina)
The Clouds
The Event
La Grande
The One Before
The Regal Lemon Tree
Scars
The Sixty-Five Years of Washington
Sanki Saitō (Japan)
Three Demons
Olga Sedakova (Russia)
In Praise of Poetry
Javier Serena (Spain)
Attila
Last Words on Earth
Mikhail Shishkin (Russia)
Maidenhair
Sölvi Björn Sigurðsson (Iceland)
The Last Days of My Mother
Maria José Silveira (Brazil)
Her Mother's Mother's Mother and Her Daughters
Kjersti A. Skomsvold (Sweden)
The Child
Andrzej Sosnowski (Poland)
Lodgings
Albena Stambolova (Bulgaria)
Everything Happens as It Does
Benjamin Stein (Germany)
The Canvas
Georgi Tenev (Bulgaria)
Party Headquarters

Dubravka Ugresic (Croatia)
The Age of Skin
American Fictionary
The Culture of Lies
Europe in Sepia
Fox
Karaoke Culture
Lend Me Your Character
A Muzzle for Witches
Nobody's Home
Thank You for Not Reading
Ludvík Vaculík (Czechia)
The Guinea Pigs
Antoine Volodine (France)
Bardo or Not Bardo
Post-Exoticism in Ten Lessons, Lesson Eleven
Radiant Terminus
Jorge Volpi (Mexico)
Seasons of Ash
Eliot Weinberger (ed.) (World)
Elsewhere
Ingrid Winterbach (South Africa)
The Book of Happenstance
The Elusive Moth
To Hell with Cronjé
Ror Wolf (Germany)
Two or Three Years Later: Forty-Nine Digressions
Words Without Borders (ed.) (World)
The Wall In My Head
Xiao Hong (China)
Ma B'ole's Second Life